THE DAY THAT I DIE

THE DAY THAT I DIE

A Novel of Suspense
P. F. KLUGE

THE BOBBS-MERRILL COMPANY, INC.

Indianapolis/New York

Copyright © 1976 by P. F. Kluge

All rights reserved, including the right of reproduction
in whole or in part in any form
Published by the Bobbs-Merrill Company, Inc.
Indianapolis   New York

Designed by Nancy Dale Muldoon
Manufactured in the United States of America

First printing

LIBBRARY OF CONGRESS CATALOGING IN PUBLICATION DATA

Kluge, Paul Frederick, 1924–
    The day that I die.

    I. Title.
PZ4.K6755Day   [PS3561.L77]   813.5'4   75–30871
ISBN 0–672–52190–3

To my mother and father

CONTENTS

PART ONE

ONE	The War Hero	3
TWO	A Country Newshawk	32
THREE	Stragglers	58
FOUR	To the Marrow	69

PART TWO

| FIVE | A Night in Koror | 127 |
| SIX | The Bone Hunters | 157 |

PART THREE

SEVEN	On Geisha Lane	179
EIGHT	Do You Believe in Love?	197
NINE	Dead Heat	220
TEN	Epilogue	240

Peleliu, Babelthuap, Koror, and the rest of the Palaus are among the more than 2,000 Micronesian islands captured by the United States from Japan in World War II. Since 1947, the islands and their people—now more than 100,000—have been administered by the United States as a United Nations Trusteeship. For the past six years, Micronesian and American representatives have been attempting to negotiate a new political status for the Trust Territory. Whether these negotiations will lead to independence, commonwealth status, or outright assimilation into the United States has not yet been determined.

Although this novel draws on Micronesia for much of its landscape, atmosphere, and mood, it remains a work of fiction, and any resemblance to real people, living or dead, is coincidental.

If Death were a man that we could see,
We would twist rope for his outrigger,
We would tie up the world . . .

Who can escape him?
Now one goes here: now one goes there
In order to escape Death,
And if we go in a circle,
Then Death knocks us down . . .

If Death were a man that we could see,
We would twist rope for his outrigger,
We would tie up the world.

From the *Dance Song of Death*
(Palau Islands—1908)

PART ONE

ONE
THE WAR HERO

I

Red Elwell kept returning to places he had been, visiting people he had known, because it gave his life the appearance of symmetry and order. Or so he believed. His wife and his sons had thought otherwise: that it was arrested development, regression, failure to advance, all disguised as nostalgia.

So they did not accompany him, and he had grown used to traveling alone—to reunions and banquets, anniversaries and memorials, old-timers' days of all sorts, where others who felt as he did came together in groups, mingling war memories and postwar regrets.

Every year, as the returns diminished, he spent more time traveling alone; the men who waited for him at airports were fewer and busier, the testimonials more perfunctory. A whole generation was shutting down.

But that didn't stop him from traveling.

Above Los Angeles, a 747 sliced through smog and dusk and began carrying Red Elwell across the Pacific.

He was the only passenger in the heavily upholstered first-class lounge. He declined the movie, waved off the roast beef carved at his seat and the tossed salad prepared on a cart in the aisle. Dismissing all services, he turned off the overhead light and sat back in his chair, rigid and still, eyes open and staring, like a dead man in need of two pennies to weigh down his eyelids.

The four stewardesses made a tiny cave of light in one corner of the compartment, chattering and playing cards.

Elwell already knew what Hawaii had become. He waited for the next plane in the airport cocktail lounge, quietly sipping a beer. Down the bar, tourists enjoyed sugary concoctions decked with pineapple slices and floating orchids. The bartenders wore leis. They looked like Filipinos.

The next flight was different—every seat taken, each one but his by a tired, numb serviceman. Honolulu to Guam to Manila to Saigon: no more slow troop transports, Mr. Roberts. Now the boredom of a month at sea was distilled into a boring twenty hours on a plane. Essence of boredom. The stewardesses flew you to your battlefield in a night, and back home just as quickly. No more temporary graveyards, fields of wooden crosses left behind while the war swept on to new islands.

Next to Elwell sat a black private, asleep, wearing earplugs, pumping the Top Forty into his dozing, warbound brain. We precious few, we band of brothers. "Heard it through the grapevine."

This wasn't his war, Elwell knew, no open-ended life-and-death struggle, everybody in it "for the duration." In Viet Nam, it was thirteen months of limited risks, in and out. Beat the clock and win the prize: a job, a car, girls who take birth control pills, and a blessedly anonymous homecoming.

Or it was "zap" and "sorry 'bout that."

Elwell relaxed a little a few hours out of Honolulu. Now, he knew, it was beginning. He could feel it, feel their presence seven miles below him, spots of land in a dark sea, passing beneath.

He would be over the Marshalls now, crossing Kwajalein Atoll, with Eniwetok to the north. To the south, the Gilberts. And Tarawa.

Down, down below the moonlight and the clouds, below the shadows the clouds cast on the sea, were the low reef-rounded atolls. He thought back to the last time he had seen them—all burned off and smoking, palm groves shredded to broomsticks and dust mops.

He thought about landing craft and passages through reefs. How he had once glanced over the side, down through the water, and been amazed to see an ocean floor plated with gold. The shell casings off the cruisers, not yet rusted.

Another hour, and they would leave the Marshalls for the Carolines, flying over the Truk Lagoon, "Japan's Pearl Harbor." Bombed, shelled, but never captured; leapfrogged and left to starve. He had visited Truk after the war, and to this day was grateful no Americans had had to push their way through one of the handful of gaps in the barrier reef, only to fight their way from mountaintop to mountaintop inside the broad, deadly lagoon.

The plane shot across the Pacific directly to Guam, flying over the islands in haste, at night, ignoring them. They were too small, too obscure now, to be called to the attention of sleeping soldiers on their way to a new war. Yet for twenty-five years the very thought of flying west, toward these islands, had moved him inexpressibly, even when the flight had broken at Las Vegas, or Los Angeles, or Honolulu. He loved the sense of westward flight, into a vault of sunset.

"Colonel Elwell? Red Elwell?"

After eighteen hours of almost total silence, of drifting over date lines and time zones and wars, a man had called his name, had found him browsing in the tax-free airport gift shop, among items he would never purchase: blotchy tapestries of the Kennedy brothers, gaudy aloha shirts, and what appeared to be a giant crab—mounted, lacquered, and labeled "Souvenir of Guam."

The man who called him was a middle-aged American in a florid short-sleeved shirt, chino trousers, and crepe-soled canvas shoes. Out of uniform, Americans made awkward colonists, Elwell thought. Except that Guam, as the liaison officer rapidly volunteered, was no colony, but an outright American possession. The slogan of the island was "GUAM: WHERE AMERICA'S DAY BEGINS." When the dawn sun crossed the Pacific, this was the first piece of American territory it warmed.

The man in the shirt—Evans—asked what arrangements Colonel Elwell would require in the five hours before the plane down to the Yap and Palau islands departed. A tour of the island? A gander at the B-52's out at Andersen Air Force Base? A few drinks at a private club in Tamuning, where Saturday night had not yet turned into Sunday morning?

At last, Evans indicated he had a bottle in his car. That was the problem with an alcoholic reputation, Elwell concluded. Not that people thought you drank, but that they assumed it was up to them to supply your drink, or take it away. They became your proprietors.

He had his own supplies, he told Evans. And he preferred to just wait at the airport for the Palau plane. Alone.

The Manila-Saigon flight vanished. The gift shop

closed before the plane left the runway.

Only Elwell remained behind at the deserted airport, sitting on a smooth concrete bench, a paper cup of scotch in his hand, beneath a sign which repeated the slogan of the island: WHERE AMERICA'S DAY BEGINS.

Now it was close to dawn. Across the runways, he could see a colony of vintage Quonsets, ugly makeshifts thrown up overnight during the war, but mellowed now with leaks and rust and screens with holes. Souvenirs.

He ran fingers through his hair, passed his hands over his face. A self-caress. And an apology, for he was truly sorry about the things he had done to his body, the stuff he had poured into it, the things he denied it, the hours he kept, the distances he traveled. It had deserved a better deal.

Elwell groped inside his suitcase for his toilet kit. He took out his razor and toothbrush, then followed the signs—English and Japanese—to the airport men's room. He thought: Today is the first day of the rest of your life.

The names diminished, and Elwell's expectations grew. Los Angeles. Honolulu. Guam. Yap. Palau. And, in the Palau group of islands, Peleliu. Like the lens of a camera, opening onto a wide-screen vista and finally narrowing to focus on a single stone. From all the world, one island.

Elwell closed his eyes. He felt the plane's slow descent toward the island of Yap, an interim stop of twenty minutes along the way to Palau. The plane flew low over the airstrip. The pilot wanted to make sure no pigs were napping on the runway.

The night before, Elwell had only felt the islands

below, sensed them as specks of land lashed by sea and moonlight. Now an island was a quarter of a mile beneath him, heaving from side to side as the plane circled. He saw the cobalt sea—nowhere in the world was it deeper than in this Marianas trench—suddenly run up against the mud-colored coral reef. Between the reef and the land was a shallow lagoon, its deeper pools walled by arrow-shaped rock fences, fish traps which looked like underwater signs pointing in toward mangrove swamps and land.

The fields around the Yap Airport were still pocked and cratered by bombs. Scattered through the surrounding meadows were parts of a dozen airplanes, mostly Zeros, caught on the strip and grounded for good. Here and there a propeller glinted in the brush, the fragment of a wing protruded out of stalks of cane. Maimed birds, shattered flight.

So the war had deposited its fragments across the islands, just as Elwell had left parts of his life behind on them. At least, these fragments had not been sold for scrap. He wondered why the Japanese had not been through these meadows—scavenging, cannibalizing, melting Zeros into Datsuns.

After Yap came Palau, the end of the line, where the plane would land, and turn, and go back the way it had come.

Contented, Elwell lost himself in the clouds and the sea between Yap and Palau. Flying over land bored him, for then a plane was nothing more than a speeded-up Greyhound, with more miles between terminals. But above islands, a plane became an aerial boat—a true seaplane—and the flight was a voyage. Seen from a distance, scattered clouds could be islands, and banks of clouds could be mountain ranges, imaginary landfalls, new continents. On a plane, above islands, you could still believe that there were real differences in the world.

The stolid DC-4 dipped a little, and, far to the right, Elwell glimpsed a wall of dark clouds and, beneath them, the green coast of the Palaus. First would come rolling, unkempt Babelthuap. Next to it, dusty, crowded, tin-roofed Koror. Fifteen miles to the south, beyond a regatta of uninhabited limestone islets, was the island Elwell knew best: Peleliu. Coral hills and pockmarked beaches. Peleliu. It had always reminded him of an egg, poaching on a hot salt sea, blistering into hills, oozing yolks of sand. Peleliu, and the end of his journey. His island.

II

Thomas Dunbar, District Administrator of Palau, watched the DC-4 pass over Babelthuap airstrip, cross over Koror, execute a slow, clumsy turn above the port of Malakal, and point itself toward the bumpy, rain-washed asphalt of what snickerers called Goding International Airport. Goding, for a departed Kennedy-era high commissioner whose administration had funded the project. "In Goding, we trust," the Micronesians had punned, but they placed much less faith in the engineering of his chief memorial: after every rain, the red clay hill collapsed and eroded; new ridges, bumps, and rises appeared in the runway; and half the public works crew was tied up for weeks at a time, its ministrations no more effective than the fresh shaking-out of a pillow under the head of a patient with a broken back. So much for the Kennedy years in Palau.

Dunbar watched the massive carrot-topped American celebrity nodding to the stewardess as he left the plane. It was hard for Red Elwell to be unobtrusive. But the man who followed a group of Japanese tourists down the line to where customs officials had placed a wooden table on the runway seemed to withdraw from public notice. Elwell's last visit, in the early Fifties, had been different. He had come to publicize *Blood on the Reef,* a war movie based on his Peleliu exploits. The distad remembered how Elwell had burst out of the plane as soon as photographers were ready, how he had made a long survey of the Palauan landscape and then passed down an honor guard consisting of two dozen local policemen, elected magistrates, hereditary chiefs, and a bone-dry fire engine. Now Elwell waited patiently for the Japanese to clear customs.

"Thanks for sparing me the leis," Elwell said to Dunbar as they walked toward the car. "They make me feel ridiculous."

"I thought a cold one at the hotel might go down better," Dunbar said. "You're welcome to stay with us at the house, though."

"Hotel's fine," said Elwell. "Junket wouldn't be a junket if I couldn't run up some bills. What's going on over there?"

Dunbar followed Elwell's glance. Near the umbrella-sized thatch shelters which shielded visitors from the sun, a dozen Japanese were accepting the formal greetings of some elderly Palauans: flower leis, bows and handshakes, protracted picture-taking.

"I had a cable about that," Dunbar said. "Those are Japanese who were associated with the Japanese administration of Palau. If I remember, we've got a former agriculturist and a police chief and a head clerk. And one of those women is supposed to be the widow of the last Japanese distad. My predecessor, you could say."

"So the Japs are coming back," mused Elwell, comparing the elaborate welcome for the Japanese to his own nondescript return. "Who are the Palauans?"

"Mostly members of the Sakura-kai group. 'Cherry blossom.' Japanese-Palauans, or Japanese-speaking Palauans, or Palauans who worked for the Japanese back then. Or want to do business with them now."

"I thought that Japanese couldn't do business in the Trust Territory. That it was off-limits."

"They can't," said Dunbar. "Not out in the open. But there's lots of willing fronts."

"I'll be damned."

Dunbar took Elwell by the arm and headed him toward the car. Maybe this was going to be a more trying visit than he'd anticipated.

Driving down the runway, past the plane, past the bombed-out Japanese communications center that served as a baggage claims area, the distad let his wife carry the conversation, and kept his thoughts to himself. He, too, was struck by the deference with which the Palauans greeted the Japanese, the little formalities and gestures they never used in their dealings with him. He sometimes wondered whether he might return at the end of another era, just as the Japanese colonials were now returning. And he speculated about how he would be welcomed, for he could not picture any of the Palauans he knew waiting for his plane to land. Not after years of boredom and drinking and fishing and philandering could he see his Palauan friends on the airstrip, waiting for him.

From the red-clay uplands at the airport, the distad's Oldsmobile followed the gravel road down a winding slope, toward the mangrove swamps, the mud flats, and the sea. Here and there, in a clearing at the side of the road, surrounded by makeshift gardens and countless outbuildings, were Palauan houses—roofed with tin, wooden-walled, with open windows and doorways.

Washlines were everywhere, with bright-colored clothing hung out like paintings. Sitting on the smooth polished floors, or on straw mats under trees, were the Palauans themselves—ragtag kids waving at passing cars, heavy, slow-moving women in print dresses, and men who were neither hostile nor friendly. It was a plane day, and the plane had landed; their expressions seemed to say: So what?

III

Later, whenever Thomas Dunbar pictured Red Elwell, he saw him as he had found him at the Royal Palauan Hotel, the morning after his arrival in the islands. The night before, the distad reception honoring Elwell had passed in record time, as if everyone concerned—Palauan and American—consented that a good distad reception was a fast reception. This one had ended so quickly that Juanita Dunbar had suggested setting up future buffet lines along the driveway leading up to the house, so guests could turn off the main road, brake at the reception line, motor past the buffet, eat in their cars, and go beeping off into the darkness, balancing plates of seconds on their dashboards.

"You know, the arrangements for your visit weren't spelled out in the cable I received," the distad remarked after the other guests had left. "Matter of fact, if someone were to press me real hard, I'm not sure I could give a lucid description of your mission down here, Red."

"Did anyone press you?" Elwell asked with a laugh. Sitting in a chair at the edge of Dunbar's lawn, he watched the last sunlight drain out from the rock islands, watched the whole flotilla of gold-green islands turn into black silhouettes. They stretched from Koror, down below the distad's house, all the way to Peleliu, fifteen miles distant.

"Hell, no one pressed," Dunbar answered. "You wouldn't either, if you lived here. Christ, after four foreign administrations, the Palauans are beyond caring who washes up here. They come and they go. U.N. Mission, Marine Corps General, Peace Corps, Department of Interior task force on this, study group on that."

"But you're wondering," Elwell said.

"Professional curiosity. And personal."

"I just wanted to come back," Elwell shrugged. "Had to." He looked across at the distad, the two of them almost in darkness now, cigars glowing, Dunbar's wife shouting cleanup orders somewhere inside the house. They could hear the police department jeep pull out of the driveway and begin lurching over potholes back to town.

"You know," said Elwell, "maybe I came back for the same reason you always had to stay."

"*Had* to stay? No one twisted my arm."

"You know what I mean."

The distad nodded, not because he was sure he agreed with Elwell, but because he felt he wanted to. He didn't know himself why he'd remained in a sleepy backwash of the Department of Interior, presiding over a sluggish custodial government of displaced bureaucrats, besotted castoffs from the Bureau of Indian Affairs, beefy ex-marines harpooned by local girls, miscellaneous misfits, and island lovers. But he had stayed, and he had had to stay, and if he was not Palauan—and he refused to deceive himself in that respect, to fall into the Peace Corps fallacy—still Palau was his home, and he loved his sprawling house built on Japanese foundations, the sound of his wife talking Palauan, the noise from a half dozen adopted children, barmaids' offspring, scattered around the premises.

"As far as my mission goes," Elwell continued, "a guy named Levinson calls me from Washington one morning, introduces himself as a Department of Interior staffer. The Parks and Landmark Commission—whatever the hell that is—is considering extending its program to the Trust Territory. You know—a campsite on Bikini, an underwater park in Truk, a lodge on Suicide Cliff on Saipan, markers along the airstrips at Tinian. Would I care to go out and inspect all the battlefields, report on their condition, make suggestions, and maybe help them out in front of appropriations committees? In short . . ."

"A junket," Dunbar finished for him. "And you're welcome to it. When do you want to go to Peleliu?"

"Tomorrow," Elwell said. "Can you set it up for tomorrow?"

Dunbar stepped into the lobby of the Royal Palauan Hotel. It was hardly dawn, and the ramshackle oversized Quonset was still asleep. Glasses, bottles of Kirin, and dirty ashtrays covered the bar. A breeze rustled in the hibiscus outside, blew in through the large rusty screens. And six fans revolved overhead, all at different speeds.

It was his favorite room in the Pacific.

He had almost turned down the hallway, past the common bathroom. He heard the shower dripping, saw a rat scuttle across the hall. But then he sensed that someone was behind him. He could hear breathing—heavy, rasping breathing.

He turned and saw Elwell, dressed as he had been at the reception, sprawled upon a couch on the near side of the lobby. His feet were hanging over the edge of the couch, and his unshaven face pressed against a pillow borrowed from a nearby chair.

"What's the matter, Red?" Dunbar asked.

Slowly Elwell sat up. He bent forward, sinking his head between his knees and passing fingers through his hair.

"Nothing," he finally answered. "After you dropped me off, those Japanese and Palauans were singing in the bar. When that ended, the barmaids started running around. Somebody in the next room scored, and it got pretty busy in there. When the noise stopped, the silence kept me up."

"You should have called me, Red."

"No point," Elwell sighed, reaching for a cigarette. "I've just gotten to the age where sleep is hard, is all."

"How about some breakfast at the house? I'll see they hold the boat."

"No. I don't want to keep people waiting."

The Peleliu boat was crowded. The distad regretted he had not made his own craft available, but he had planned an outing to Babelthuap that weekend. Besides, he guessed Elwell would have turned the offer down.

"You get down there, ask for the demolitions man," Dunbar said. "There's no hotel down there, not much of anything, really, only one village. But they'll put you up someplace."

"Thanks," Elwell said. "I'll be fine."

"How long will you be down there?"

"A couple days. Maybe less."

"It's not much of an island these days, Red," Dunbar said. "Lot of hot coral and rusting war surplus. Always seems about ten degrees hotter down there. And it still has that burned-over look, like a forest fire passed over it last year."

Elwell nodded, and the boat began moving away from the dock, out the Malakal channel.

"Don't forget to contact the demolitions man," Dunbar shouted. "They're clearing the caves down there, stuff you guys left behind. His name's Atkinson. He's a character."

IV

Merle Atkinson had shown up in the islands a few years before. He had come—he said with a smirk—to "clean things up."

In 1944, the northern end of Saipan Island had been used as a munitions storage depot for the planned invasion of the Japanese home islands. When atom bombs ended the war, the military administrators of Saipan were left with miles of useless ammunition. Some they shipped home. Some they dumped into the sea. But these methods were too costly and time-consuming. The administrators decided to solve their problem by exploding the surplus armory where it lay, in bunkers and revetments.

What happened was a catastrophe. Or would have been, had it occurred anywhere but on battle-scarred Saipan. Instead of exploding, the shells were scattered intact, all over the northern end of the island. The shells lay everywhere, buried in the ground, or half-buried, hidden in thickets of tangan-tangan brush, strewn along sandy beaches and at the bottom of cliffs, hurled against caves in which fallen Japanese defenders still festered.

Fenced, declared off-limits, the northern part of Saipan—Marpi, it was called—became the domain of fruit bats, deer, pigeons, and poachers. Soon the poachers foraged for more than wildlife, stripping brass and copper from the decaying live shells and selling the metal for fifteen cents a pound. At night, lights bloomed in the Marpi boondocks, the clink of hammers echoed off the cliffs, followed sometimes by the sound of an explosion.

In 1968, the United States Government ordered the clearance of the Marpi area—an act of kindness which coincided oddly with the early rumbles of American withdrawal from Southeast Asia. To remove the debris of the last war and clear the decks for the next, the administrators contracted Merle Atkinson, a retired Navy demolitions chief. There was no weapon Atkinson could not identify, no bomb he could not defuse.

Atkinson more than cleaned up the old battlefield. He probed, exhumed, and restored it, diving into submarines, rediscovering jungle command posts, climbing into cliffside caves. By the time he left Saipan, he boasted that he had turned "an overgrown scrap heap" into a "first-rate tourist attraction for Americans and Japanese alike." There were new roads leading to Suicide Cliff, to Japanese Caves, to the "Last Command Post." There were markers and peace monuments along the roads, and a flower-bordered museum at the gate, loaded with the artifacts Atkinson's crews had unearthed—helmets, boots, maps, and weapons. Atkinson, meanwhile, departed to Peleliu to work his magic on the site of one of the worst Pacific battles.

"We're having some party," Atkinson remarked as he led Elwell along a trail winding into the center of the island. The two men passed teams of Palauans chopping paths through the brush and stacking shells according to size, like archaeologists on a bizarre dig.

"There's less stuff here than on Saipan," Atkinson

continued. "But to get it, you have to go inside caves and tunnels, sliding around in bones and batshit, and you practically need a cable car to get the stuff out of there."

"Are there many people left? Down there?"

"Some. The caves that have been open for a while are pretty well picked over. You find some shoes and mess kits and small arms. Maybe a shinbone or some teeth. Your skulls are pretty rare, though, since the Japanese bone-collecting parties have been through."

"Bone collectors?"

"Sure. Bone hunters. Widows and orphans of the dead Japs. Whole bunches of 'em come on down, lookin' for poor Hiroshi's rib cage or Toshiro's bridgework. It's a pisser. We got a bunch of bone hunters camped out near the village now. They follow us around with hip boots and pith helmets. And cameras."

"And they're still finding men?"

"Hell, yes. Every damn group that comes through is supposed to be the last one, the final search, after which the place is declared free and clear, all boned out. But then, sure enough, we get another group a few months later on. And they always manage to come up with something. See, a lot of the caves got blasted shut or bulldozed when the guys inside wouldn't surrender. When we go down into those . . . well, you find anything you want. Ain't nobody left."

Elwell sat with Atkinson and his Palauan crew while they broke for lunch, camping out among the piles of weaponry.

At the corner of the clearing, a blanket was spread on the ground, as if for a picnic. It was covered with some of the larger scraps of bone the crews had brought out of the caves. Some waggish Palauans had tossed gnawed-off chicken bones onto the blanket as well.

"You want to go down into one of those caves?" Atkinson asked Elwell, passing him a beer. "I've got some spare clothes you can put on. You'll need 'em."

Elwell sipped his Kirin—it had been frozen in the morning, and there was still some ice inside the can—and declined with thanks.

"I didn't think you'd go for it," Atkinson responded. "It's a real mess down there, everything wet and dark and rotting. Don't see why anybody would want to go down in there, after all this time. Every once in a while we find one of ours. Come across a dog tag hanging on something. And I've got to decide, do I sack it up and call Guam, so maybe some family—or what's left of some family—gets to have a funeral twenty-five years late? Or do I bury it around here with no fuss?"

"What do you do?"

"On Saipan I had no choice—we were too close to Guam. Here I just take the dog tags, put 'em in a can, and leave the rest for the Japs. You think that's all right? If it was you, or somebody you knew?"

"It's just as well," Elwell answered.

After lunch, while the rest of the men got back to work, Elwell walked over for a closer look at the bone-covered blanket. It was dry, broken calcium to him, and nothing more. Twenty-five years was too long for love or hate, too late for funerals. Most of the men who had died then would be dead now, or old and ready for death.

V

Atkinson turned out to be one of those rootless, technically trained Americans who wander the world on two-year contracts but remain unchanged by any of the places they contact. He was a gaunt, red-necked, hacking-coughed Appalachian who carried the atmosphere of the strip mines, the slag heaps, the Hank Williams honky-tonk wherever he traveled.

His obtuseness drove Peace Corps volunteers on Peleliu to despair. Atkinson shrugged off whatever language was babbled by the people around him. Careening around Peleliu in his jeep, chasing girls, hurling beer cans, dynamiting fish, pot-shotting birds, he broke almost every rule of address, of courtship, of caste, of social deference. Yet he was a good man with the ordnance, and it was to his house, with its cold beer, hillbilly music tapes, and frying fish that the Palauans came at night, while Peace Corps volunteers sat alone with their book lockers and vocabulary cards.

"A few beers and an occasional piece of ass" kept a man going on Peleliu, Atkinson told Elwell when they came home that afternoon. From where he sat, outside Atkinson's house, it seemed to Elwell that his host had plenty of both on hand. The Palauans, many of them members of his crew, sat around savaging a case of warm Kirin. Inside the house, Elwell heard some girls chattering in raucous-sounding Palauan.

Then came the Japanese.

A white-painted jeep pulled to a halt in front of Atkinson's house, and three men dismounted. Dressed in white clinical-looking uniforms and wearing helmets with red crosses, they looked more like an ambulance team than a group of scavengers picking over the remains of the last war.

They did not enter Atkinson's yard, but stood smiling in the roadway.

Atkinson excused himself and, gesturing to one of the older Palauans, shambled out toward the jeep, which, Elwell noticed, was a Mitsubishi. After huddling with the Japanese, using the Palauan as an interpreter, Atkinson assembled the entire crew next to the jeep.

"Come on over," he shouted to Elwell, "and bring me a beer. They want to take a picture of the bunch of us."

Elwell brought the beer and started to step away. But one of the Japanese visitors protested.

"No, come on," Atkinson said. "They want you. They recognize you. I didn't know *Blood on the Reef* ever played in Japan."

"Neither did I," Elwell said, stepping into the picture next to Atkinson. The demolitions chief held his can of beer toward the camera man, as if he were posing for an advertisement.

"This is a daily ceremony," he whispered to Elwell. "They come to find out what caves we're workin' tomorrow, which ones are clear, and where we'll leave the soupbones. And then we all pose. I put up with it because one of 'em carries a Polaroid and the guys in the crew like to have the pictures."

"Are you sure they want me in this picture?" Elwell asked uncomfortably. "I mean . . . shit."

"Bygones is bygones," Atkinson said. "They insisted. Just keep the beer can pointed toward the camera, say 'Kirin,' and cut a fart. Our little joke."

The rest of the crew picked up the word, and the farting, as they smiled out at the Japanese, whose expressions were lost behind the clicking glass-and-metal Nikons. They all posed for minutes on end, until the ground was strewn with scraps of paper, boxes of film, tampons of fixative. At last, one Palauan cut a thunderous blast of wind, enough to curl paint and send cockroaches underground. The whole crew broke for the yard, laughing.

Elwell stepped rapidly toward his chair, anxious for another beer. He had half-downed it when one of the Japanese approached him across the yard. It was the man who operated the Polaroid. Elwell stood up, wondering whether he had arisen out of politeness or an urge to protect himself from attack.

The Japanese was smiling. Not directly at Elwell, but around him, an undirected smile, something like a letter, written, stamped, and sealed but missing an address. The Japanese extended his hand.

Elwell took the Polaroid snapshot and nodded slightly, answering the Japanese's slight bow.

He watched the jeep drive away and heard Atkinson next to him, belching.

"Another souvenir of Peleliu," Atkinson said. "Now you can show the wife and kiddies where you been."

Back at the side of the house, the Palauans were throwing a fresh load of fish onto a white-hot corrugated metal sheet.

"They don't bother cleanin' 'em," Atkinson explained. "Seems warm-water fish don't have all the guts that cold-water ones do."

Elwell stared at the fish. Whole bodies, head to tail, broiling on the metal. The fire below was uneven. Some fish burned and charred, patches of crisp meat and scales adhering to the metal. Some ruptured, almost exploded. Others stayed half-raw. No one cared.

"The Japs did that," Elwell remarked.

"What? Broil fish? They eat 'em raw, too."

"With our fliers. The ones they captured. Put them on sheets like that."

"That's a hard way to go," Atkinson said after a moment.

"They were cruel people," Elwell said, turning to Atkinson. "Don't you forget it."

Elwell napped on Atkinson's bed, falling asleep to the sound of Palauan voices and hillbilly music. It was dark when he awakened, but the sounds were the same. A nasal voice came out of the tape recorder, singing about divorce. Elwell splashed water into his face and shaved.

He stepped into the yard where Atkinson was sitting, his chair surrounded by empty beer cans. He was drunk now, red-eyed and restless.

"That's Miss Tammy Wynette, and she sure tells a story in a song," he said. "Have a beer, Red."

"Just one," Elwell said.

"Just one at a time. Where you bunking tonight?"

"The distad said you could help me out. Set me up in the village infirmary, maybe."

"Hell, I've got an empty house. You married?"

"Not anymore."

"I got a wife on Guam, but she don't like it down here. I can find us both a U-drive, though."

"A what?"

"Local expression for a girl who's not too particular who she goes with. There's some home movies inside, too. Action from the Philippines that you would not believe. And I don't mean General MacArthur."

"Atkinson, I need the keys for your jeep."

"Huh?"

"I need the keys. I want to go down to Orange Beach."

"Tonight? Now?"

"Yes."

"All right, old buddy. Keys in the ignition. You know the way?"

"More or less."

"You want me to come with you?"

"Thanks, but no."

Atkinson nodded and walked him out to the jeep.

"It's a moonlit night, so you can't get too bad lost," he said. "It's an island. Sooner or later, you always get back to where you started from."

VI

A pocket of Appalachia, Atkinson's house disappeared. Elwell passed the bombed-out Japanese building which held the village's generator; he heard the humming sound from inside bullet-scarred walls and ruptured ceilings. He saw a light here and there in the village and groups of Palauans sitting out around fires, talking the way Americans once talked, watching evenings from their front porches.

A motorbike crossed the road in front of him. The girl riding in back flicked the beam of a flashlight across the jeep.

Two girls stepped out from beside a betel palm and waved to him, calling out in Palauan. They broke off in midsentence when they saw that he was not Atkinson.

After the Palauan shacks vanished, he saw a few lights in a grassy field, saw the Japanese jeep parked beside some pup tents.

The road dipped down into a pool of mud, just barely above a mucky taro patch. The moon glazed the broad leaves growing out of the swamp.

Then he was out of the mud, climbing a little hill which brought him to a straightaway, a wide corridor of moonlight fringed by brush and soft-needled pine trees. It was the Peleliu airstrip.

He accelerated, barreling down the runway, exhilarated. He liked the speed and the feeling of the wind, which was almost cool, and he saved braking the jeep for the last possible moment, right where the runway ended.

Soon the brush encroached from both sides, tangan-tangan branches sweeping against the windshield, slapping against tires, reaching inside and rubbing against his knees. The road became a tunnel through the brush. Then it became a stream bed, impassable. He brought the jeep to a halt.

There was enough moonlight for him to find his way down the trail, but he kept his flashlight out, unlit. Parting a barrier of brush, he stepped on sand and heard the sea.

He looked up and down the beach. To his side, he saw the dark, square shape of a landing craft. Across seven miles of silver water, he detected the island of Angaur, too flat and low to form a silhouette, but betrayed by the blinking red light on the tower of the Coast Guard station at one end of the island.

He walked between the dry sand and the waves to the breakwater, climbed over a wall of rocks, and had at last come to his destination. Los Angeles to Orange Beach.

Protected from the open sea by twin arms of rock, it seemed the harbor had been sheltered from time as well. Had Elwell come by day, he would have noticed the rust and the heat, the ships and tanks decaying in piss-warm water, impaled on rocks, buried in the sand, or half in half out of the water, like paralyzed amphibians. He would have seen the wreckage left behind by more recent visitors—campsites and beer cans and empty boxes of film. And he could not have missed where the scrap-metal dealers had cut and stripped.

But alone, at night, he dealt in shapes, and silhouettes, and memories. He was surprised by how similar were the docks and ships and breakwaters to what he remembered of the place, as if the quarter of a century between visits amounted to nothing more than the transition from high noon to full moon.

Memories. They should have come easily, but he had used them all up. What he remembered was blurred and tangled, like when you hold not one but two or three slides together against a light.

Memories of Peleliu, memories of the film they had made, memories of stories he had told a thousand times, and stories he had never told.

Once, it had been the most important island in the world. When it was taken—its airfields captured, its ten thousand Japanese defenders slaughtered—MacArthur would be free to invade the Philippines, to go wading into history. That was in August 1944.

Even then, Peleliu had seemed too small a place to figure in such a vast design. Eight square miles of land. Before the invasion, a friend of Elwell's had calculated that, with a full marine division on shore, there would be one man for every three square yards of land. Whatever happened on Peleliu would be over quickly, they had thought.

"We're going to have some casualties," Marine Commander William Rupertus had told his men. "But let me assure you that this is going to be a short one, a quickie. Rough but fast. We'll be through in three. It might take only two."

After ten days of aerial bombing and three days of naval gunfire, there was a real question as to whether any Japanese on the island were left alive. The place seemed deserted. A pilot who had flown over Peleliu a day before the landings said, "It seemed like an immense broken graveyard. I looked for signs of life but couldn't see any."

The beaches were defended. There were coconut-log cradles, concrete pillboxes, tank traps, barbed-wire barriers. Mines and aerial bombs were buried in the sand. The Japanese riddled the marines with mortars during the day, attacked at night behind tanks. But the beachheads held and widened. The marines fought their way inland, capturing the crucial airfields within a few days.

That was when the nightmare began.

The Palauans called it Umurbrogal. To the Japanese, it was the Momijii Plateau. The Americans named it Bloody Nose Ridge.

Photographed from the air before the battle, the limestone hills of Peleliu had seemed green and harmless. Beginning just north of the airfield, the hills were half a mile wide, two miles long, and no more than a few hundred feet high.

Now, when shellfire had ripped away every trace of green, the ridge stood out, steep, pitted, threatening, exposing attackers to fire from a dozen directions. The ridge was the heart of the island and the key to the Japanese defense. On Peleliu there were no desperate rushes, no costly banzai charges. For the first time in the Pacific, the Japanese retreated in order, disappearing inside the mountain and reappearing to fight on other—on many other—days.

There were more than five hundred caves inside Bloody Nose Ridge, natural tunnels extended and reinforced by the Japanese. The Ridge was honeycombed with passages, permitting forays and escapes in all directions. Some tunnels were nine stories high, with exits at every level, connected by stairs, barred by sliding doors. Some tunnels were half a mile long, lit, wired, ventilated. One cave alone garrisoned one thousand men.

The marines captured the beaches and the airfield and surrounded the ridge, and yet the island was not theirs.

From down below, they watched the planes pounding away at the Ridge, struggling to subdue it through beating, or burning, or bombing. Nothing worked.

It wasn't World War II. It was a medieval siege, and the Ridge a natural castle, a fortress of moats and battlements, keeps, tunnels, dungeons. Subsisting on brackish water and salt tablets, grappling with lines and slings and pitons, Elwell and the others scaled the cliffs, advancing by inches, plugging holes with flamethrowers and satchel bombs, blasting or sealing every cavity they could find.

But at night, the Japanese popped up in new orifices and reclaimed the Ridge.

On October 12, 1944, the battle for Peleliu was declared over. The airfields were under American control and the Japanese stronghold had been whittled down to nine hundred yards by four hundred.

The first attackers were replaced by reserves. Only the Japanese remained constant.

While the newcomer troops mopped up, the war moved on to other islands.

What had it meant?

At odd points, up and down times, in the ironic quarter of a century that followed, Elwell often wondered about Peleliu.

After the war, he learned that Bull Halsey had recommended that Peleliu be by-passed. America could take the Philippines without first neutralizing Peleliu, Halsey thought. But MacArthur was leaving nothing to chance, and MacArthur prevailed. The unnecessary battle had been fought.

A hero, a film star, and a public relations man. In that order. The years had cut Red Elwell down to size. And diminished his island, too. Peleliu. Who'd ever heard of Peleliu?

You could spin the globe a thousand times and never set your finger on the place.

And tonight, a wreckage among wreckage, walking war surplus, Elwell was saddened, but not surprised, at how little he felt. No great surge of memories on Orange Beach, no replay, no renewal, no more attachment to this place than to that charnel heap of bones on the picnic blanket outside Atkinson's cave.

He stayed awhile at the end of the breakwater, first looking in at the old harbor, then facing the open sea —the winking red light on Angaur—waiting for his mood to change. It did not, and he left.

He drove the jeep slowly down the runway. He noticed the cracking sound of snails crushed beneath his wheels, saw coconut crabs and rats scuttling away from his headlights.

A light—a moving, walking light—was ahead of him on the runway, signaling for him to halt.

Behind the flashlight, Elwell saw a Palauan—with a T-shirt, khakis, beer gut, and greased-down hair.

"Man hurt in the boonies with a bomb," the Palauan said. "Got to take him Atkinson house."

So they are still stripping bronze at night, Elwell thought.

He followed the Palauan off the runway, into a trail through the tangan-tangan. Far ahead of him, he glimpsed a stationary flashlight, like a distant campfire.

The Palauan moved fast, heading uphill, squeezing between rocks which marked the base of Bloody Nose Ridge. Elwell breathed hard, concentrating on keeping up.

The hand—the glove—that came from behind him covered his mouth, and, almost instantly, he missed his air.

The hand pulled him backward, turning him, spinning him off balance.

Now the flashlights were not far away down the trail. They were shining all around him.

The knife caught Elwell in his side, turning viciously between his ribs, moving and turning, searching for his life.

I will run, Elwell thought. Damn them, I am going to run.

He staggered down the trail, into darkness, but the flashlights followed him. Candles in search of a moth to burn.

My side hurts, I can feel the blood, warmer than sweat. But I am ahead. They will not touch me again.

Out of the brush, he was on the runway, staggering toward the jeep, panting.

Is that blood I taste in my mouth?

They were behind him now, with flashlights and knives, beams of light and metal rushing to converge on a single point.

He won the race to the jeep. He had a hand on the

wheel and a foot inside the jeep and was hoisting himself up when the man inside turned on a flashlight of his own, blinding Elwell. Then someone grasped Elwell's head by the red hair, and Elwell felt the knife enter below his ear, felt it slice across his neck, and just had time to look down, amazed, at the transformation of his chest.

TWO
A COUNTRY NEWSHAWK

I

"All right. Whenever you're ready, shoot."
"You want the punctuation?" Booker asked.
"No, I'll dub it in later. Just start talking."
Marshall Booker thought he detected some resentment in the clipped, overprofessional instructions that came to him from the other end of the line. The poor soul rolling a sheet of copy paper into an Underwood was probably bridling at Booker's privileged status and resented being pressed into taking dictation on a weekend morning. Nonetheless, Booker began to dictate:

"I told myself, I said, 'You've got to be kidding,'" muses film director O'Dell Duchamps, recalling the genesis of his most controversial undertaking. "A black version, a black *musical* version, of *Wuthering Heights?* Set in Kentucky? With Brock Peters and Cicely Tyson? But the more I played with the idea, the more it played back at me, played with my mind."

That is how *Breezed Off*, which blows into national release over the holidays. . . .

He dictated rapidly and listened to the New York typist struggling to keep pace. A barely audible "Jesus Christ, Booker!" hissed at him from across the continent.

Just when the typewriter seemed caught up—he could hear it going into upper case for the quotation mark—Booker began again, spinning it out. The effortless, facile prose that earned him a living.

He could count some blessings this Beverly Hills Saturday morning. ITEM: the sun splashing into a forty-eight-dollar-a-day room in the nouveau-Mexican wing of the Beverly Wilshire Hotel. ITEM: next to the complimentary fruit basket, a pre-publication copy of his second book, a collection of journalistic pieces, already listed as a Book-of-the-Month Club Alternate. ITEM: the splashing sound of water from the bathroom where Jill, a sandy-haired fellatrix from La Jolla, was rinsing out the night.

Idly, Booker leafed through his note pads for quotes to strip into the third graph. ("Shit, quote me as saying anything, man," his subject had said. "You're in the business, I'm in the business. We both want our name in print, right?") While he read words into the phone, his California girl emerged from the bathroom, not yet dressed. Still talking to New York, he motioned her back toward the bed, and down toward the birth of another new-journalistic legend, not the first from Marshall Booker.

Possibly there are still some dissenters—grumbling potbellied alcoholics who wear green eyeshades and work nights—who do not accept that the field of journalism has stars who, by force of personal style, enhance whatever subjects they touch. But the proposition has been often, and elegantly, demonstrated. Ask publishers, ask editors, ask the very same hacks who take dictation on Saturday mornings, muttering to themselves, *"I* could look as good as Booker if I had *his* kind of assignment."

Like it or not—and enough people who mattered had learned to like it—Marshall Booker was a celebrity-journalist. Talking through a lead story by phone while a brunette was anchored between his legs was mere ornament on an established, and carefully cultivated, reputation. For Marshall Booker had buried psychotherapy, flying lessons, mobile homes, and his own divorce proceedings in his expense account, had vacationed in the middle of wars and covered wars while on vacation, had ghostwritten major policy speeches during political campaigns, and then himself had leaked the advance text. All of which, he cheerfully conceded, was "middling good for a country newshawk from a little town this side of Amarillo."

Along with a dozen other writers schooled on southern or southwestern newspapers, Booker had come north in the early Sixties at a time when New York publishers and editors—hidebound academicians, bookish semites—were anxiously discovering America. What they discovered was Marshall Booker: his country-store manners, his courthouse prose style, and his endless backlog of big stories from little places.

Unkempt, pin-striped, picturesquely disorganized, Booker moved from office to office, the embodiment of "local color," purveying his pieces of Americana. There were profiles of cryptofascist football coaches, aging cowboys, peculiarly articulate Klansmen. There were pungent forays into minor sports: coonhunting, cockfighting, pit bulls, rodeos. There were landscapes of small towns and big ranches, roadhouses and cathouses, high-school reunions, last roundups, and third-party political conventions. And above all—certainly larger and longer-lasting than any of his float-right-off-the-page story subjects—was Booker himself, definitely roughshod and definitely successful, a kind of Will Rogers of American letters.

It took Booker a while to leave his country-boy colleagues behind, but it happened. For where they remained local colorists, begging for another assignment that would carry them home, back to the Panhandle or the Delta, back to their private Yoknapatawphnas, Booker fashioned his country persona into a whole new meal ticket, gaining access to movie locations, campaign trains, missile launches, and locker rooms. Big-league locker rooms.

Two years before, a publisher had collected some of Booker's pieces in a hardcover volume entitled *Down Home*. A preface written by a New York columnist-novelist hailed Booker as "a master writer masquerading as a journalist . . . a refugee from both newsroom and classroom." Now had come his second collection. *One Night Stands*, it was called.

Now, when Booker covered a story—he glanced down at Miss California, bobbing for apples in the Garden of Eden—he *became* the story. By his very arrival, he transformed and glamorized what was waiting to be reported. He was like an anthropologist who discovered forgotten tribes; but for him, his people would remain in dark caves.

Another glance down, a few more words to New York, and Marshall Booker completed his dictation.

II

The phone call from Edmund Shank was a pleasant surprise.

For half an hour, Booker had been alone in his hotel

room, wondering whether to return to New York or parlay a few more stories on the coast.

Booker had never met Edmund Shank but had always hoped to. Shank's magazine, *Gotham*, would be the last outfit in New York to want his stuff, he warned himself, and he meant just that. Not that they might *never* use him, only that they would be the last to do so. Because he feared a frosty rebuff, because his regular outlets kept him plenty busy, Booker had never approached Shank. Who needs it? he thought.

Still, he had sometimes cast a longing eye at *Gotham*. Whatever they thought of his work, he liked theirs. *Gotham* had class. The Jackie Onassis of magazines.

Under Shank's management since World War II, *Gotham* was one of the few surviving magazines which did not have a demographic hang-up or a stylistic formula, did not sandwich beaver pictures between the lesser work of dead or used-up writers, did not sprinkle words around pictures or pour them into layouts which were conceived before a story was even written. It was not a glossy, narrow, special-interest magazine for hook-and-bullet freaks, singles, blacks, dune-buggy fanatics. It was not tucked into Sunday newspapers, nor was it deposited next to flight-sickness bags in airline seats. *Gotham* believed, or was said to believe, that there was no substitute in journalism for putting a good man in the field with enough time to cover an important story right. It was a threadbare, marginally profitable credo. Booker had heard they were in trouble. Now he had his proof.

Shank did not sound like the sort of editor who worried about advertising and circulation. But then, they never did, not even on the day they folded and TV crews showed up to film pictures of their final issue going to press.

"We've got a piece we thought might be right for you," Shank began. "But you'll have to start immediately. And it's open-ended. We don't know how long it might take. Months, possibly. And it involves a lot of travel. We're offering our top rate for the piece and a substantial kill fee if it doesn't work out. Are you interested?"

"I most certainly am," Booker answered promptly. Now is not the time for my head-scratching country act, he told himself.

"I'm sure you know the name of Lewis 'Red' Elwell? A World War II hero in the Pacific?"

"The Audie Murphy of the Pacific," Booker answered. "I sure do. A sad case these days, I hear."

"Even sadder this morning. He's dead."

"Bound to happen, the way he was drinking."

"Not quite. He was murdered. Bayoneted, actually. Repeatedly bayoneted. And it happened on Peleliu, in Micronesia, the same island he fought on in the war."

"What was he doing out there?"

"According to the newspapers, he was on some sort of survey trip," Shank said. "No arrests yet. The islands in the vicinity of the killing have been cordoned off, evidently. We'd like you to go out and follow the investigation."

"I see. Sounds interesting. It's different, all right."

"Let me add this, Booker. We're not interested in a whodunit, though that, obviously, is an element which will have to be confronted. Rather, we're taken with the pathos of a man's returning to a place where he was a young hero and dying there. The changes in the place. The changes in the man. You can begin it in the islands, but you may have a good deal of research to do in the States after you return from Micronesia."

"Micronesia." Booker chuckled ingratiatingly. "It's out of the way for me."

"Out of anybody's way, I should think," Shank said. "But you have a chance to do an insightful piece. Red Elwell—the name had a lot of resonance once."

III

Resonance, indeed. By the time Booker reached Honolulu, the newspapers were full of Elwell. There were obituaries, sidebars, tributes, and battle pictures that looked like stills from *Victory at Sea*. Not surprisingly, the retrospective pieces, perfervid eulogies from wartime buddies, and summaries of the struggle for the Pacific took up most of the newspaper space.

There were some mordant notes, however, in the accounts of Elwell's postwar career. The stories charted a slow decline, from war hero to hero of a war movie, to unsuccessful political candidate—he had lost in a congressional primary. From there, Elwell became a "public relations counsel"—flack—for a defense contractor. After that, he was a "spokesman"—subflack—for Rio Seco Developments, an Arizona realty company which plunged into Chapter XI bankruptcy proceedings in 1956.

It got worse. In the late Fifties and early Sixties, the "Audie Murphy of the Pacific" had become the white Ira Hayes. Drunken driving reports cropped up, and there was a lawsuit, settled out of court, resulting from a punch-out in a Los Angeles restaurant. A TV pilot—"Under Fire"—had bombed in 1963, and two years later, Elwell was divorced.

The last anyone had heard of him was eighteen months before his death, when an enterprising feature writer discovered that Elwell's oldest son, Keith, had skipped to Canada to avoid the draft. Dried out and surprisingly sympathetic to his son, Elwell had posed for a picture at home. It showed him sitting in a folding chair outside a mobile home in the San Fernando Valley.

There are no surprises in this man's life, Booker thought. It peaked early and declined abysmally, without even a temporary victory, a momentary reversal, along the way. Without even a note of protest from Elwell against the downhill direction of it all. The dead war hero reminded Booker of the boyhood friends he met on his returns to Texas, the fellows he had described—vindictively, they claimed—in one of his better pieces, a story about a high-school reunion back home in Amarillo. It told how the glorious hardscrabble athletes, the splendid back-seat ass-men of his youth, had succumbed to their jobs and years and marriages. And it was not—he had written—it was not just that they had aged, that they had grown fat, that their hair had thinned, but that their whole expectation of life had diminished. There is only so much wildness and heroism in a life, they seemed to say; it only peaks once, and if your peak comes early, then the remainder will be all downhill.

None of this explained Elwell's death, of course. Here, the newspaper accounts were bare bones: the location of Peleliu, its previous connection with Elwell, his reappearance there on a government-sponsored tour. There were comments from the Palau District Administrator, the Trust Territory High Commissioner, and a demolitions expert on Peleliu, the last man to see Elwell alive. Well, not quite the last, unless Elwell had developed a middle-aged curiosity about hara-kiri.

Booker was surprised the newspapers had run a photograph of the dead Elwell, for it was worse than the worst car accident. He was collapsed on the front seat of a jeep, one hand through the steering wheel, head against the dashboard, and blood everywhere, down his neck, over his chest, down his legs.

In other pictures, you could follow the whole life that had led up to that moment in the jeep. The scrappy recruit mugging it up in boot camp, the combat shots in the Pacific, the decoration by MacArthur, the homecoming parade in Portsmouth, Ohio. You could see him posing in front of a model home in Arizona, stepping out of a courtroom and, last, or next to last, sitting in the sun in front of his trailer, a year and a half before the pig-sticking on Peleliu.

IV

"Yes, we take his death seriously," the marine officer intoned from the front of the room. "And we have ample reason to do so. Elwell was a fellow marine. He was an American. And he was a guest in these islands. We all take his death seriously."

Booker yawned. The press conference on Guam hadn't netted a single scrap of additional news about Elwell. He looked around at the poor drudges who were transcribing this treacle into their notebooks. He recalled the old newspaper joke about updating news stories: "Still dead this morning is Red Elwell, who . . ."

The TV crews, who had flown a long way for some dull footage, seemed especially dispirited, sensing that, though their cameras were focused and their microphones plugged in, something vital was lacking. As usual, they were stupid, childlike in their trust in equipment and in the ability of that equipment to precipitate news. Lights, camera, action. But it was not working, not with Major Scott Beckman. They were striking friction matches against a bar of perfumed soap.

"And we are seeking the support and active cooperation of Trust Territory officials, Palauan leadership, and any other agencies or individuals capable of contributing their resources to this investigation," Beckman droned on.

His sentences tumbled out, clause taped to clause, everything already printed on the handout presented to reporters as they had entered the room. Thick, wooden phrases, deliberately unquotable, typed in capital letters, triple-spaced, and smelling deliciously of mimeograph fluid.

"Peleliu has been completely isolated," Beckman said, finishing a paragraph.

"Hey, was that hard to do?" a reporter wisecracked.

"Can you get there from here?" another asked.

"What's going on down there? Or is it up there?"

"The island—it's seven hundred miles south of here—has been completely cordoned off for the duration of the investigation," Beckman answered calmly. "We control movement on the island, off the island, and *to* the island."

"You mean you won't let us go there?" the first reporter burst out combatively.

"Glad to have you come," Beckman replied. "If you want to fly down there at your own expense, and stay, at your own expense, you're welcome. Of course, there are no hotels, and you'd have to rough it."

Booker laughed out loud. The third day of a two-day news story. It would take the discovery of Amelia Earhart taxiing over Guam, of Martin Bormann cooking a helmetful of fruit bats in a Peleliu cave to bring this group back to life.

V

Beckman was amused.

"These must be parlous times," he said, "when a magazine like *Gotham* sends you all the way to Guam on a missing-person yarn."

"You know me, Major. I'm a circulation builder."

"Circulation builder? Hearstian word! Only a couple years ago they broke down and listed their writers in the table of contents. Now they're recruiting the likes of you to build circulation!"

"This Elwell thing—actually, it's not a bad story."

"Come on! *True* or *Argosy* . . . not *Gotham.*"

"*Argosy* wouldn't touch it. Not after that numbing press conference you gave this morning. Did you write that crap yourself?"

"It served the purpose," Beckman answered. "I can hear typewriters clicking shut all over Guam. Except yours. Did the folks at *Gotham* give you a deadline, by the way, or do they abhor the phrase?"

Booker shook his head. "All the time in the world."

"I thought so. I can't picture *Gotham* thinking in terms of deadline. I see their writers inscribing stories in longhand with a quill, scattering sand over the manuscript, and sending their stuff in book rate."

Booker had always found Scott Beckman an anomaly among military men, not only in Saigon, where he had been known for—but never damaged by—his sardonic appraisals of "the progress of the war," but in New York, on leave, when he rambled in bookstores, attended concerts, and showed an insatiable love of theater.

Wherever they had met, Booker liked the man. Beckman was something special. It showed in his delectation of odd phrases, in his willingness to take risks in conversation, to be an ironical half stroke off in his choice of words, in his cultural tastes.

When Beckman shed his uniform—as he had this evening, for dinner in an Agana steakhouse—he was not stripped of his identity, like so many military men —a cipher suddenly in search of an integer. There was another man, just as good—a poised, tanned, confident civilian underneath. Booker had always seen a lot of himself in Beckman: the country boy traveled far from home, the cunning, cultured hick, smoothly roughshod. They were two of a kind, Booker thought, and that spelled friendship.

"Well, now, you ain't seen much of the island," Beckman said after dinner. "And to tell the truth, there ain't much of an island to see. But you're here, I'm here, belly's full, sun's goin' down, girls just now comin' out. Let's get 'em before they pee."

VI

"Now we got us legal cockfights on weekends, and they tie some real miracle blades onto those roosters' spurs, just like home. We got three civilian movie houses, air-conditioned. And there's a seedy pugilistic pipeline up from Cebu City, so we see something that's alleged to be boxing every couple weeks."

Beckman interrupted his drawling narrative to sip some scotch from a peanut butter jar he kept in his glove compartment. They were meandering along Marine Drive, the shore road circling Guam.

"Num, num. Want some Skippy? Duck down when you sip. There's cops. Now on your right, that's the A & W root beer stand. We got a McDonald's down the road some. Pox Americana. Now you stop me soon's you have any questions. You sure look puzzled."

Booker was puzzled. It disconcerted him, moving

through this landscape of pastel gift shops and enamel gas stations, past yards of junk cars and tracts of concrete-block houses. Had a tidal wave swept across America? Had it dislodged every fly-by-night business, every flimsy structure, every cheap idea and washed them up on beaches around the world?

"Didn't they find a Japanese straggler here last year?" Booker finally asked. "Sergeant Yokoi?"

"They sure enough did, standin' right in line for a double whopper at Burger King Saturday night. Never did have a chance."

"Come on!"

"Okay, okay, I've answered more damn questions about Yokoi. We've got thirty thousand military on Guam. About a third of the land is in military use, the navy at one end and the B-52's on the other side. Then there's Agana and Tamuning and a few other towns all in one clump, a regular Ellis Island loaded with Guamanians and Flips and Micronesians. That's what we're driving through now. A pony-league Honolulu. But there are boondocks. Want more?"

"How much Johnny Walker can you fit into a peanut butter jar?" Booker asked.

"Never empties. It's a true miracle, ordered by mail from a late-night radio station in Del Rio, Texas. Now Yokoi—you were asking about Yokoi. He lived out around the back side of the island, which we're coming into now."

"Farming country?"

"Now that would be a stretcher, Booker, that would be going some. They shoot some semi-wild cows when they need food for a baptism or a three-day wake. And there are coconut crabs and papaya around. Papaya goes good with salt, chasing beer. And on moonlit nights they *say* they go hunting crabs, but it's mostly an excuse to go out and get laid. But it's too hot for farming, so long as there's jobs around bases or hotels. Which is why an industrious Japanese homebody could last a quarter of a century out there. Funny, too, when you think about it. This island swarming with Japanese tourists—mainly honeymooners—and that old buzzer from the Imperial Army out seining shrimp in the Talafofo River."

"He reminds me of Elwell," Booker ventured from behind the peanut butter jar. "Elwell with a twist. One man leaves the battlefield, returns to it, and is killed. Another lingers behind for twenty-five years and is finally captured—rescued—and thrust into the new Japan. Both stragglers, in a way."

"Kee-rist, Booker, I can hear them slamming the rewrite button already. A tale of two stragglers."

"It's not that bad. It might work."

"Yeah, for Classic Comics. You gonna go down and report the story anyway? Or does this wrap it up?"

"A formality. Once you get your lead paragraph, everything else falls into place."

"Well, here's a candidate for your finale," Beckman said. "Something to wind up your yarn."

He turned off the paved highway and drove down a dirt lane, past several mammoth Quonsets. From the motley-colored washlines, the rusted cars in front, the raggedness and disrepair, Booker guessed that the Quonsets had passed from military to civilian occupancy. Loitering in doorways, gambling and drinking, were dozens of Filipinos, contract laborers at nearby installations. But it was not to these men or these buildings that Beckman pointed.

Set back from the road was a square, two-story wooden dwelling circled on both floors by a wide, open porch and splashed from roof to foundation by gaudy pink paint.

The Pink House was swarming with Filipinos. Wiry, sullen men sat on the steps chatting. Some were throwing knives at a fallen coconut. One fondled a fighting cock.

Then Booker saw something that shocked him. He had guessed that the Pink House was a brothel, had reasoned that there must be such an outlet for an army of displaced laborers. But then, not once, but several times, he saw men step to the front of the porch, unzip their trousers and—cigarette in hand, still bantering with their countrymen—proceed to relieve themselves on the grass below. Except that they were not urinating. Their hands pumped methodically, building speed and rhythm, till relief came.

"When they go inside, they want the bitch to work," Beckman commented. "They want their money's worth."

"Never saw anything like that in Mexico," Booker said.

"Keep in mind that you're less than three miles from where they found Sergeant Yokoi. Now you can use this little tableau to end your story."

"In *Gotham?* They wouldn't print it."

"They should. Those guys are the real stragglers. Not the guys the war leaves behind. The ones who follow her, wherever she goes."

"The women inside . . ."

"Woman. I doubt if there's more than one. It's not much of a knock shop."

Beckman turned at the end of the road and headed back to the highway.

"Say, Magellan landed somewhere the hell around here in 1521, before the Flips knifed him. You want to see if we can find the marker? Or hit a few bars back in town?"

VII

It reminded him of a roadhouse in his home country, from the cars and motorcycles parked in the front yard, straddling shards of broken beer bottles, to the semihostile youths idling around motorcycles, to the Country and Western music that came pounding out from behind screened windows.

"Where are we anyway? What decade?" asked Booker as he squeezed between a brace of Datsuns and moved toward the door of the Tiger's Cage.

"You expected, perhaps, teahouse of the August moon?"

"This scene is out of the Fifties."

"Optimist. Wait'll you see the jukebox."

The girl who brought them their first round of drinks began to sit down at their table, but Beckman waved her away with two quarters for the jukebox. From where they sat, they could take in the whole transplanted American scene—tables of young men, out of uniform but obviously military; bar girls winding from table to table, no more than slightly pleased or mildly annoyed by the hands that reached out for a tug on their breast or a pat on their ass; a jukebox and a pool table and a long bar, decked out with Slim Jims and cheese snacks, potato chips and pretzels; over it all, the voices of Hank Williams and Jim Reeves and Loretta Lynn, sounding poignant and exotic at this distance from home.

"Don't misunderstand. There are black bars, too," Beckman was saying. "You wouldn't be comfortable there."

"They have bar girls, too?"

"Hell, yeah, same as here."

"Are these available?" Booker asked.

Beckman paused, inhaled, and began.

"Sure, they're probably available, if you want to drink till 4 A.M., wait outside in a car for another half an hour while they clean up in here and decide who's going with who, and then sneak off to some rusted Quonset—that's if she comes through—step over half a dozen relatives sleeping on the floor—and then, with maybe one hour before sunup and your lady not too fresh, yeah, sure, you can do it. You might even get in for free. 'Course you can piss for nothing, too, and do it now."

"You've learned the hard way?"

"I know about military places."

"Just what the hell is in the Pacific for you anyway? I had you figured for Washington. Or maybe Cambodia, if you stayed overseas. Not Guam!"

"Don't be fooled," Beckman answered. "Guam is the center of an interesting ball game now. With the withdrawals from Southeast Asia—you remember Southeast Asia?—this whole Pacific region is coming alive. Guam you know about. Tinian and Saipan, just north of here, are heating up. And there's lots more strategic real estate—and all the problems associated with obtaining it—in the Marshalls, Truk, Palau. No end of problems."

With that, Beckman stopped. Booker waited for him to resume, just waited, but Beckman gazed silently at the roomful of young American beer drinkers, as if he were foreseeing other rooms in other places.

"Snap out of it," Booker said.

"I just told you about the easy part of my job."

"There's more?"

"That depends."

"Come on!" Booker said.

"Word gets out on this, I spend the next fifteen years checking hemorrhoids at Fort Dix."

"I'm not taking notes. Hands off."

"You've heard about My Lai . . . what the guys did over there?"

"Everybody has heard about My Lai."

"You heard about *one* My Lai. There were lots of 'em," Beckman said. "A bunch of 'em. Fact is, our late crusade produced between one hundred and one thousand men who cannot be permitted to return to the United States right now. We call 'em the My Lai guys."

"Why? What've they done?"

"Well, some—as the name suggests—have been involved in, associated with, what might be alleged to be war crimes."

"You're talking like a lawyer."

"I *am* a lawyer. That's one of the reasons I got this shit detail. Anyway, these guys returning stateside would embarrass us and get entangled in publicity and court proceedings. We'd be forced to court-martial them. So we hold them here on Guam for special disposition."

"What the hell is special disposition?" Booker interrupted.

Beckman ignored the question.

"Besides the boys with legal problems," he continued, "there are others who are plain crazy. Send them home and they'd take their discharge pay, buy a rifle, climb a tower, and bang away. Then there are guys with physical problems. You've heard all those scare stories the army feeds recruits? About incurable diseases, venereal and otherwise, and if they catch 'em, they can't come home? Well, it's not just something we made up so's they'd remember to wear rubbers."

"You keep them here?"

"The whole bunch. We chose Guam because it's out of Asia but it's not America. It is American territory, though, and that can be advantageous in the case of certain discharges."

"What do you do with them?"

"Some good and some bad, I guess. The psychiatric cases, for instance, get plugged into some of the best treatment that money can buy. Ditto the guys with diseases. We hold 'em and work on a cure. Sometimes, if they want it, we arrange to put their names on casualty lists, dead or missing in action. Sometimes, for some of the guys who do well, we set up a new I.D. That's hard."

"How about letting your old buddy visit the My Lai guys?"

"Impossible."

"But you're on the staff."

"And that's where I want to stay. I breeze in with you, I'll be an inmate. Nobody gets close to the My Lai guys, and they get close to nobody. Believe me, that's a fair enough deal."

"No favors for me?"

"Not on this one. But there is another favor I had in mind. A phone call to a lady who wants to meet you."

"Hey, that's not necessary."

"The hell it's not."

"Don't go calling around . . ."

Beckman lifted his hand, raised one finger.

"One call," he said, "is all. No calling around. One call. Would you not do the same for me if I came to your island?"

"A pro?"

"No amateur," Beckman said. "But no fee, either. There's a standing arrangment to accommodate VIP's. Can't have 'em out watching B-52's come in all night."

They drank while they waited, but the drinking changed—two lines which had converged now crossing and moving away from each other, disappearing into separate planes. Beckman became more cautious, more deliberate, while Booker accelerated. One good act of folly deserved another.

And they bowled, bar bowling, metal puck, and sawdust, flash-o-matic, shooting down an alley to where the red light sped in front of the pins, and Booker winning, fitting right into a perfect groove, strike after strike, the accuracy and the timing and the rhythm all together, like a rehearsal for professional sex, till Beckman tapped him on the shoulder.

"Inez doesn't speak much English," Beckman said, and introduced them.

"My God!" Booker whispered as they walked from the bowling machine to their table. "She's incredible. She's Suzy Fucking Wong!"

"And she's yours, Booker. I can tell she likes you, right off. And she's dying to get to know you."

"No, no kidding around. That's no piece of ass, that's a . . . my God!"

"No argument at all," Beckman cheerfully agreed. "You say she's not a piece of ass, she's not a piece of ass."

The Inez whom Booker seated at the table was as beautiful a woman as he'd ever seen. Whatever Guam lacked, whatever it could never be—Tahiti, Hawaii, Bali, Shangri-la—Inez amply was. She had the facial features, eyes, and cheekbones of an Oriental, but instead of the chinalike fragility, small bones, and pale skin, she was tan and full, straight black hair cascading down over her shoulders, reaching all the way to a breathtaking bosom.

Trying hard to steady himself, Booker looked hard for a flaw, something that was less than perfect, something to brake his enthusiasm. The test failed.

While Beckman ordered a fresh round of drinks, Booker groped for conversation, flattening complicated sentences into simple English.

"Are . . . you . . . from . . . Guam?" he asked.

"Not born on this island, on Ponape Island," Inez answered. "Father Guamanian, mother from Ponape."

"Do you . . . do you like it here . . . on Guam?" Booker improvised, blushing at his own banality.

"Okay here, but want to see Hawaii sometime. Maybe I go there soon. My sister, she stay at Honolulu."

"Honolulu is . . . a much bigger place . . . than Guam. Than here."

"Yes."

He could see Beckman yawn like a bored chaperone, and he felt embarrassed himself, as if it were his fault that he couldn't find the words to reach her. For her part, Inez seemed good-naturedly patient with his trivial questions, and this made it worse.

"Is . . . Ponape Island . . . like Guam?"

Puzzled, she shot a stream of Chamorro at Beckman, who quickly answered in kind.

"There are only one movie on Saturdays in Ponape," she began, "and not good like Guam. And the roads are not good. Very full of holes."

"Aah, I *see*," Booker answered, enlightened. The waitress—a slovenly, slit-dressed slattern, pregnant—finally arrived with their drinks. From the way Inez stiffened in her chair, Booker sensed that she was not a regular in the Tiger's Cage.

"Your English is good," he resumed.

"No, not good, only a little."

"Did you learn it on Guam?"

Inez never had to coin her answer. She was saved by

the drink Booker tipped over the table, ice cubes and all, flooding out the colony of pistachio shells Beckman had been neatly stacking.

While Booker sputtered apologies, looking in vain for the waitress, he heard another exchange of Chamorro between the other two. Now it was Beckman's turn to speak.

"Say, Marshall, it's been interesting, but she's wondering if you wouldn't like to do something now, before you've had any more to drink."

Her hand was on his leg.

"Can you drop us off, back at the hotel?" Booker asked.

This time, there were two exchanges, initiated by Inez.

"Hotel's no good," Beckman explained. "She doesn't want to be seen going into a room there. You understand."

"Sure. Well . . . is there room at your place?"

"Out of the question. The night has a thousand eyes, and most of them belong to military wives."

"Well, what will it be then?"

Something—it sounded like a suggestion—from Inez.

"Why don't you kids step out to my car? It's parked way at the side of the lot."

"The car!"

"Why not?"

"Beckman, this girl needs sheets and pillows and showers and . . ."

"She suggested it."

"But I haven't done it in a car in fifteen years! At least!"

"So? I'll wait inside. And no rush."

"Jesus, Beckman, I've *never* done it in a car."

"It can be done, friend, and Inez is willing to teach you how. I hear there was one time she went up in a helicopter . . ."

"I don't want to hear about it."

"Your move."

There were no choices, Booker realized. And besides, her hand was moving.

They stood up and left the table.

"There's a tape player and some cassettes under the dash," Beckman called out from behind them. "Mantovani; Blood, Sweat and Tears; Jim Croce. Upbeat, mood, take your pick."

Incredible, Booker thought, walking between crowded tables, through clanging guitar music and hot, smoky air, a yard behind the fine and nonchalant Inez.

Outside the Tiger's Cage was the same roadhouse tableau—the grass lot full of cars, the stolid youths with cruel faces. Booker waited for them to make a remark, just one crack. . . . But the youths had nothing to say.

The two of them zigzagged between parked cars, to the dark corner of the lot where Beckman had parked.

Had he known that they would be using his car?

Booker opened the rear door for Inez, and she got in.

VIII

A gray dawn in the tropics. Rain on the hotel patio, on colorful beach balls and surfboards, on the wings of B-52's coasting home after a night's work in Asia, rain on the sea itself, wasted rain.

An ashy ocean slapped impatiently against a flat white beach. Palm branches which had shone like emeralds in the sunlight turned into drab metallic tendrils, umbrellas in a mourning procession.

Booker awoke and thought about Inez. He wanted more of her, more than a couple of jumps in the back of a car parked outside a beer joint, with Beckman waiting inside, like the square kid whose father loaned him the family wheels.

He thought about bringing her to Honolulu when this Elwell story was over. Why not a fling in New York? Men had made worse deals with women.

If he were not working for *Gotham,* he would kill the story now and have her with him on a plane tonight. He could practically write the Elwell story now, anyway. What did it really matter anyway? Who cared how Elwell wound up?

Inside the passenger terminal at the Guam Airport, Booker looked out at the rain and waited unenthusiastically for the Palau plane. He was not hung over and he had not been sick, but he was in a state of stasis, of absolute neutral quietude, which meant that he had stopped drinking just one drink short of a hangover.

He could easily have remained where he was sitting all day, watching Palau passengers queue up for boarding passes. Escorted by affluent-looking relatives who lived on Guam, the Palauans trailed cardboard boxes of carry-on luggage and clutched their little blue Trust Territory passports like poor people hold food stamps at a grocery counter in a good neighborhood, fearful of being turned away.

It was scarcely ten o'clock, but he already felt an afternoon nap sneaking up on him. The hand on his shoulder jarred him like a blowout awakening a drowsy motorist.

"A little shaky this morning?" Beckman chirped. He was brisk and cheerful, back in uniform. Any discomfort, any exhaustion from last night would be charged against another account, an alternate civilian body.

Booker responded sluggishly, suddenly tired of their

Butch Cassidy–Sundance Kid camaraderie.

"Why are *you* up?" he asked Beckman. "I have to be here."

"So do I. Preparations for the ceremony. A Coast Guard flight is bringing Elwell up in a little while. You'll be gone by then."

"Are you helping to hang the bunting?"

"Crepe. Anything else I can do for you on Guam?"

"Haven't you done enough?"

"Some mink, huh? You think she's fine, check out her big sister in Honolulu on your way back. I can set it up."

"Thanks. More than kind of you."

"Okay, the man in charge of the investigation on Peleliu is Colonel Anthony Vincent. A real pistol, a scholar in uniform. He'll be at the airport, arranging for the shipment of the coffin at that end, and he'll stick around and wait for your plane. You can go down to Peleliu with him. If you still want to go. If not, there's a Honolulu flight this afternoon."

"No," said Booker joylessly. "It's time to go to work."

"You sure? No telling what they'll come up with down there. Colonel Vincent takes his time on everything he does—sort of fellow you could order to drain Lake Erie with an eyedropper. All your buddies are covering the ceremony here and following the body home."

"That's their kind of story," Booker said.

"Okay, okay," Beckman said. "Your contact is Colonel Vincent. And you might look up the district administrator, Tom Dunbar. Been in Palau since the dawn of time. A little island-crazy, but he knows the territory."

"What's it like down there?"

"You'll miss Guam," Beckman said, walking away. Then he stopped and turned.

"Say, Booker?"

"Yeah?"

"You *did* get the lady's phone number?"

Booker nodded and waved. Already, he looked forward to returning to Guam.

It was still raining lightly, but the sky was brightening, and people began to come out of the airport buildings. Crepe was being draped around the airport, knots of military officers were drinking coffee. Elements of an Armed Forces' band tumbled out of a bus. Guamanian families, early arrivals, pressed against a retaining wall, one of them bearing the island's all-purpose banner, WHERE AMERICA'S DAY BEGINS. And from one of the hangars came the sounds of a platform being hammered together. All preparations for Red Elwell's melancholy homecoming.

But it was clearing up nicely, and it didn't look like a sad day at all.

THREE
STRAGGLERS

Life on Peleliu had been comfortable for Merle Atkinson. Days of work around the caves with a crew of men he had hired and trained were followed by nights of drinking and sex. On weekends there were fishing and boating, obscene picnics on deserted beaches in the Rock Islands, forty-eight hours without a stitch.

But that was over. Since Elwell's killing, Atkinson's life on Peleliu had been shattered, and he doubted that he could ever put it back together, not even if Colonel Vincent found his band of killer-stragglers tomorrow.

With work suspended during the murder investigation, Atkinson had nothing to do. He listened to his tapes, which bored him the way a jukebox which starts repeating itself bores an all-night drinker. Atkinson drank more, and he drank alone. Members of his crew did not drop by to drink with him, no one brought him fish, and his girls had gone home to stay.

Desperate, Atkinson asked Colonel Vincent for permission to leave Peleliu, to visit his wife on Guam. The request was denied. The marines would need his guidance when they searched the caves. Then he asked permission to bring his wife from Guam to Peleliu. Request again denied. There were killers loose on the island, Colonel Vincent said.

Now, grouchy and headaching, Atkinson picked his way through the encampment on Orange Beach, the base of Colonel Vincent's search-and-destroy operation. The marine who had hammered him out of his midday nap pulled back the flap of Vincent's tent and let Atkinson step inside.

Seated at his desk, the colonel studiously puffed his pipe and ignored the visitor.

This isn't a camp, Atkinson thought. This is a movie set, a goddamned costume drama. Here's the command post. Spread out on the table you have maps, charts of Peleliu, jars of salt tablets, books of military history. You have sketches of the cave system. You have divisional histories, stacked like yearbooks, in one corner.

Outside the tent, through a narrow slit in the canvas, Atkinson glimpsed the thing he missed most of all, its absence signaling all the changes that had come over Peleliu. Draped with plastic sheets that reminded him of an oxygen tent—his impounded jeep.

Colonel Vincent finally noticed him.

"Under the weather?" he asked.

"Weather sucks," Atkinson answered. There was nothing like being retired from the military.

"Sorry to hear that. Anything I can do?"

"Lots. But you won't."

"We've been over that before, haven't we?"

"Yeah, we've been over everything. So why do you want me now? Is today D-Day?"

"There's a man here I want you to meet. He's a reporter for *Gotham.*"

"For what?"

"*Gotham.* That's a magazine in New York, and he's here to do a story on Red Elwell."

"I don't take any magazines," Atkinson answered sullenly. "Take too long to get out here. Arrive with covers off and pages out."

"*Gotham* isn't one of those. I want you to cooperate with Mr. Booker and tell him all you saw the night you found Elwell."

Atkinson didn't especially like the tall, expensive-looking civilian who stepped into the tent bearing a tape recorder and a can of soda. He talked country but he looked city.

"Atkinson is one of our most valuable resources in this project," Colonel Vincent was explaining. "Apart from his detailed knowledge of the cave systems at the center and north of the island and his standing within the indigenous community . . ."

"Not so good with the indigenous community lately, Colonel," Atkinson interrupted. "I'm sitting around with my cock in my hand while you get ready to replay World War II."

". . . he was the last man to see Elwell alive and the first to see him dead. And since that's our point of departure, I thought you would want to hear about it all from the primary source, rather than by way of the summary in my report—which will be made available to you as soon as it's been duplicated."

"Christ, not again," said Atkinson, combing fingers through his hair in search of his headache.

"Mr. Booker will appreciate your cooperation in this request. And so will I."

"But I've been through it all with you. You tape-recorded it."

"Just one more time," Colonel Vincent said.

"You'd be doing me a big favor," Booker chimed in.

"Do I owe you any 'big favor'?" Atkinson asked hopelessly.

Booker turned to Colonel Vincent, who was rekindling his pipe expectantly and waiting for the tale to begin.

"You don't have to sit through this, Colonel," the reporter said. "Not if you've already heard it. Just leave us huddle together for a while . . ."

"Really, I don't mind," Colonel Vincent said.

"But certainly there are other . . ."

"No, no, I'd like to audit this session. If *you* don't mind."

"No, not at all," Booker lied.

He tested his tape recorder, pushing forward and reverse buttons, telling the machine where he was and to whom he was talking, stacking spare cartons of recording tape on the table.

"To tell the truth, the first thing I worried about was my jeep," Atkinson began, "and it started as soon as I saw Elwell head down the road through the village. When he asked me for the keys, it was like getting to Orange Beach that night was the most important thing in his life. There was no saying no to him. But as soon as he left, I started thinking about where he was going. Not the getting lost so much as the holes along the road, the washouts, the shoulders, the trees that come down after every blow. Nobody takes care of all those roads, nobody ever did, and they change every week now. I figured him a sure bet for a broken axle. I had another beer while I thought it over. I tried to shake it off. He's a pro, I told myself, he knows what he's doin', where he's goin'. But I didn't believe it, and the more I thought about it, the less I believed it. After maybe forty-five minutes of farting around, I decided to go after him. Not that I felt good about it—I figured that they were his private memories on that beach, and he had a right to 'em. But it was *my* jeep he was drivin'.

"Some of the guys from the crew were still around the house, and among us we had a half dozen motorbikes. That's how a lot of people get around here. I borrowed one from a fellow who was stretched out drunk, some of the others got on theirs, and we took off like a damn posse, laughin' and shoutin'.

"We really barrel-assed it out there. We got to where the road goes up and down and back up and feeds into the end of the old airstrip. That's when I saw my jeep."

"Hold it right there," Booker said. "This could matter a lot to me. I want you to picture it all—everything you see when you try to remember the scene on the runway."

"Well, the first thing for sure was my jeep. I could see it way down the runway, stopped, with the lights still on. I remember thinkin', he's had a flat, that's all, and hopin' that's all it was. And startin' to worry that maybe it was something more, like a rock had knocked a hole in the gas tank, or he'd banged the axle. Or gotten it overheated from runnin' too hard, though that would be impossible, almost."

"That'll do," Colonel Vincent interrupted. "The possibilities for damage to your jeep were infinite. But there was nothing wrong with it, as it turned out."

"Not much," Atkinson muttered, "except for the stiff in the driver's seat."

"Continue, please," Booker said. "You're doing fine."

"Am I?" Atkinson asked. "Well, the headlights were on, like I said, but there was more light than that around the jeep."

"More *light?*"

"Yeah, more light than the headlights would make, more than you could account for that way. There were a bunch of other lights around the front seat, smaller lights than the headlights, all blurred together."

"You couldn't make them out? Distinguish between the different lights?"

"No, not from that far away. There was a pretty good moon that night . . ."

"Three-quarter moon," Colonel Vincent interjected.

". . . and you could see pretty good all around, but as soon as you hit the pool of artificial light around the jeep, you lost the moonlight and it all blurred."

"Okay, continue."

"Well, the bunch of us headed down, maybe slower than we should have. I thought, there's a problem with the jeep, but what's done is done, and it looks like he's already got help, so no point in stormin' down there and makin' him feel extra bad about the damage. So we started off slow and regular down the runway. I'm sorry about that now."

"Why?" Booker asked.

"Well, because I guess that's when they were gettin' done killing him."

"Tell it in order, please," Colonel Vincent insisted. "You didn't know that then. Just tell it exactly as it happened."

"Well, the closer we got . . ."

"Just a second." It was Booker's turn to interrupt. "I want to make sure I have all of the initial scene—everything that met your eye when you and the others drove your bikes onto the runway. So far, I see the jeep and the illumination around the jeep from the headlights and the other lights. Anything else?"

"Not that I . . ."

"Visualize it. Close your eyes."

"I don't need to close my eyes. I remember."

"What do you remember?"

"My jeep. And the lights. And the moon."

"That's all?"

"Just the runway, like you'd see it tonight. About eight hundred yards of macadam, old macadam, weeds popping up all over, crappy little saplings breaking through the cracks. Then, behind the jeep, a line of taller trees where the boondocks begin. Inland would be the start of the mountains. Umurbrogal."

"What was that last word?"

Colonel Vincent intercepted the query. "Umurbrogal is the Palauan word for the hilly area. The marines called it Bloody Nose Ridge." He spoke through a cloud of pipe smoke, clearly pleased that his scholarship had paid off so soon.

"I see," Booker said. "That's all there was."

"Everything else that was there then, you could see there tonight," Atkinson said. "Except the moon."

"Then what happened?"

"We drove down the runway slow and easy, but our lights were on and we weren't hiding from anybody. So they saw us coming, I'm sure of it. And then the lights broke away from the jeep. Flashlights or torches, I don't know."

"You mean they went out?"

"No, they . . . you know . . . scattered, dispersed. Instead of being clumped together 'round my jeep, they were headed off away from it, toward the boondocks, moving fast. And then the only lights I was looking at were the headlights from my jeep, and I followed them right along, like goin' up a driveway."

"Then?"

"I pulled up by the jeep and found him. Elwell."

"Was he dead?"

"Yeah, he was dead, but just barely. He was still bleedin' all over himself, and I think there was sort of a shaking spasm in the leg that hung out the side of the jeep. But he was dead, all right, no doubt about it. Fresh killed."

"Did you touch him?"

"I just leaned over and looked in at first, till I was sure he was dead. Which didn't take long. Then I touched him. And I moved him."

"Why?"

"There was . . . I saw that one foot hanging outside of the jeep, just getting done shaking, and I decided to pull all of him into the jeep, 'stead of just leaving him hanging there, half in, half out. I got in the other side, hooked my hands in his armpits, and pulled him up onto the seat."

"Understandable, under the circumstances," Colonel Vincent conceded.

"Then what did you do?"

"I asked one of the Palauans to drive back to the village and get on my radio and tell the Coast Guard station at Angaur and Dunbar—he's the distad—to tell them that Elwell had been murdered and that we needed help here."

"That's when our involvement began," Colonel Vincent said.

"Then I did a foolish thing," Atkinson resumed. "I saw Elwell dead and bleeding in my jeep, and the lights carried by the men who killed him were moving away from us, pretty far away now, but you could still see them. And there I was with five, six men on motorcycles. I decided we'd go after them. They were armed, I knew, and we weren't, but I thought we might get lucky and pull one down. Or at least see where they were going. I just wanted . . . to make things harder for them.

"We fanned out and headed after them. As long as we were on the runway, we gained fast, and we did okay on the lateral roads through the flatlands. We really did some biking that night. It must have surprised them, thinking they had it in the bag, their job all done, and then finding a damn motorcycle gang on their ass, and gaining. We did gain on 'em, too, for a while."

"How close did you come?"

"At the closest, a hundred yards."

"Could you tell much about them? Who they were or how they were dressed?"

"No, all I could see was they were men and they were running, and I knew that already."

"Why did they keep their lights on?"

"That I do know. Once you get into the boonies, running under trees, cutting through the brush, you need a light to see your way. There's all kinds of holes and trenches and craters; it's hard enough to get around in there during the day. And at the bottom of the Ridge, which is where they were headed, the terrain really goes crazy—ravines, gullies, roots, branches, broken coral that can cut you to ribbons. That's what stopped us in the end. Soon as we hit the slope, we started losin' em. And we'd come so close! It was like we'd tried to cup our hands around some fireflies, but every time we brought our hands together, they flew a little higher, the bastards. Then I saw them headed up the mountain. It was slow going for them. But it was no going for us."

"Why?"

"They had it made. Home free. That mountain is like Swiss cheese, tunnels and caves they could duck in anywhere, stay inside, come out someplace else. Or just sit back and lay for us."

"So they disappeared on the mountain?"

"Right. The lights came together one last time, then went out. And there we stood, watching. And all I could do was stand there and shout 'fuck you' up at 'em. Which I hope they heard; it echoed up and down the Ridge. And I just then noticed that during the whole run from town and up the mountain, I'd been carrying a beer in my hand. Full can. I meant to bring it to Elwell to show him it was okay about the jeep, whatever happened. I remember I threw the beer up their way, heard it bang against a rock and come rattling down, along with some loose stones. That's all."

The warning buzzer sounded from the tape machine.

"Let me change tapes," Booker said.

"Save it," Atkinson answered. "That's the story. The Coast Guard came over in no time. The next morning, the marines landed."

"You forgot the patrol," Colonel Vincent interrupted. "You always forget it."

"Oh, yeah," Atkinson said. "After we lost them in the caves, I made sure some guys stuck around the Ridge. Others patrolled the beaches and the roads. Nobody got off the island that night, I guarantee you."

"So that's why you're sure that whoever did it is still here?" Booker asked Colonel Vincent.

"Exactly."

"Then it looks like you succeeded in making it harder for them, Mr. Atkinson."

"Harder for myself, too."

"Just one more question," Booker said. "The tape's off, and that's okay. Who do you think they were? Or are?"

"I don't know."

"I didn't ask that. I know nobody knows. I asked who do you *think.*"

"I don't think Chief Atkinson is in any position to speculate about that," Colonel Vincent said. He tapped his pipe against an ashtray as if he were pounding a gavel. "All we can ask him for is his account of what he knew and saw, which is what he has given. The rest is for us to find out—with his help, when we get to the caves."

"I can go now?" Atkinson asked.

"Yes, and thank you," Colonel Vincent replied.

"I'll need a ride back. As you well know."

"Dobbs will drive you."

"And some rations. I'm running out."

"Dobbs will take care of it. You're welcome to lodge down here, of course. You're part of the team."

"Thanks. No, thanks."

Atkinson nodded at Booker and left the tent, squinting as he stumbled into sunlight.

FOUR
TO THE MARROW

THE FIRST DAY

The next morning, before dawn, the hunt for Elwell's killers began.

Booker heard the camp awaken, sounds of boats plowing out of the harbor, jeeps coughing into life, messages crackling from the communications tent. All that was missing, he thought, was the sound of overhead bombers and offshore gunfire softening up the enemy.

Colonel Vincent was finishing a substantial breakfast when Booker stepped into his tent. The colonel was lighting his pipe, first step in a day full of judicious thinking and carefully considered statements.

"Everything on schedule?" Booker asked.

"According to plan," Vincent answered. "Not that I expect to come up with anything the first day or two. The search of the southern part of Peleliu is *pro forma*. We won't get warm until we hit the caves."

"Are you going out to have a look?"

"We'll take a helicopter ride in a little while. But first, I wanted to talk to you."

"Fine. What about?"

"About me, for one thing. On Guam, what did they tell you about me?"

"They told me you were scholarly. And thorough."

"They were being abnormally kind," Colonel Vincent chuckled. "If it were up to my fellow officers, the majority would vote to have me committed tomorrow morning."

"Why's that?" Booker asked. He was feigning an innocence and a sympathy he did not feel. From their very first meeting, Vincent had impressed him as a boring ass. Oh, he was scholarly, all right; he practically wore elbow patches on his fatigues. But his scholarship was at the total mercy of an obsession: a fascination with the dates and details and personalities of World War II. The military's last big hit.

There was another problem, too. Going out of his way not to be a roughneck, a drill-instructor type, a "Toughie" or a "Chesty" or a "Brute," Colonel Vincent rushed to the other extreme. He revered the free press, asked admiring questions about heavy-thinking pundits Booker rarely even read. He loved words like "candid" and "forthcoming." He reviewed Booker's questions before he answered them: "good question," "penetrating," "well put," and "insightful."

"The reason I'm considered an 'odd duck,'" Colonel Vincent said, waggling his fingers to form quotation marks around "odd duck," "is that for years I've entertained certain theories which, as it happens, will be tested during the next few days here. I think I should explain those theories to you now."

The picture of cooperation, Booker flipped open his spiral notebook and braced himself to take notes. Courtesy notes. He did not expect Colonel Vincent to come up with anything worth quoting, but he knew the colonel would appreciate attentive transcription of whatever he said.

"Begin with this."

Colonel Vincent handed over a yellowed piece of paper, a photograph that had once been an illustration in a magazine—a Japanese magazine, to judge from the caption. The picture was of a Japanese officer, middle-aged, grayish crew cut, sad eyes. In his expression it was easy to read the premonition of defeat.

"We never knew the Japanese we fought," Colonel Vincent said. "The Germans were different. They had . . . flair. They were memorable people. In the course of a war, you developed a sense of what they were like as individuals. You could relate to a Rommel or a Guderian. Even a Dönitz or a Kesselring."

"The bad guys."

"Perhaps. Villains, but personal villains. Worthy opponents. If you captured them, you'd want to talk to them. Or read their memoirs. By comparison, the Japanese were an impersonal tide. The yellow peril, numerous and anonymous. When we pictured their leaders, we pictured stereotypes. Fu Manchus in uniform."

"Who's this fellow?"

"Sadao Inoue. The general who fortified Peleliu, planned its defense. And turned what should have been a quick fire-fight into the worst battle of the Pacific. Take a good look at him, Booker. He was one of the best they had. And—in a sense—it's him we are still fighting. His fortifications, his cave system, have enabled Japanese to remain here for twenty-five years."

Booker looked, nodded, and handed back the scrap of paper. He began scribbling in his notebook. He scribbled garbage. Messages to himself. Chronological listings of women he had known. Lists of sexual positions.

"You figure some Japanese are still inside the Ridge?" Booker asked. "Stragglers?"

"It's the surest thing I know."

"How's that?"

"Item one." Colonel Vincent spoke as if he were giving dictation. "In November 1944 an army colonel stepped off a transport at the airstrip here. And was instantly killed by a shot through the head. That is a matter of record.

"Item two. In February 1945 five Japanese dug themselves out of a cave and went on a marauding spree around the island. That, too, is in the records.

"Item three. In 1947—*seven*—when the American garrison here numbered eighty, including some dependents, a raft loaded with stolen rations was found floating in the swamps here. A warehouse was looted. A marine sentry who fired a shot was answered with rifles and grenades. What's more, there were signs that Japanese stragglers from Babelthuap were coming down here by boat."

"Very well. But has there been anything since then?"

"I understand your skepticism," Colonel Vincent said, relaxing a little. "After 1947, the record gets skimpy. In the early Fifties the Palauans caught a couple of stragglers robbing a taro patch, and that's the last confirmed report we have. But that's not important. There are no reports because there were no Americans here to make reports. And the Palauans wouldn't make a fuss unless someone was killed. The Trusteeship began in 1947, and the military pulled out of here."

"But not the Japanese, you think?"

"Exactly! Look, Booker, I'm not trying to sell you anything. I'm asking you to look at the facts—and the possibilities—realistically. Palau was an unnecessary, desperate, botched-up campaign. On paper, we won it. But victory and defeat are relative terms. Only in the sense that Peleliu was effectively neutralized as a basis for Japanese counterattack did we win it."

Colonel Vincent waggled his fingers again to make

invisible quotation marks around the word "win."

"I also reason that if there were any island in the whole Pacific likely to sustain a substantial number of Japanese stragglers, it would be Peleliu. Because of its small native population. Because that population—unlike the Filipinos or Guamanians—had no special enmity toward the Japanese. Because the Americans pulled out altogether, not like Guam or Okinawa, which were transformed into massive bases. And—most of all—because of the cave system, which no one pretends was completely penetrated or effectively sealed off."

"All right, but why did they kill Elwell? You're not suggesting, are you, that they *recognized* him?"

"Of course not. But he was in an unlikely part of the island at an unlikely time. He might have been just crazy enough to light out after them in that jeep. And it may also be that the Japanese have been rattled by the work that Atkinson and his crew are doing in the caves. They might be losing their hiding places."

"All right, maybe you have something," Booker said, snapping shut his notebook.

"Good," said Colonel Vincent. "Now, let's hop that chopper."

There was nothing subtle about Colonel Vincent's strategy for the recapture of Peleliu.

From the helicopter that hovered over the southern end of Peleliu, Booker could see long lines of marines stretched across the width of the island, combing the beaches, beating the bush, wading through coastal swamps with guns over their heads. At sea, patrol boats kept pace with them. And there were even groups of men swarming over tiny offshore islets.

"The whole search strategy replicates the wartime

capture of the island," Colonel Vincent said with a touch of pride. "We'll move off the beaches, take the airfield, outflank the ridge. We'll march up both sides of the island till we join forces in the north, encircling the cave system. Then we'll have some action."

"Just what is the status of those stragglers? You consider them combatants? Or criminals? Or war criminals, or what?"

"That's unclear. But I doubt if it will make any difference. Let's take a look at the Ridge."

They passed over the airstrips, three connected runways forming the numeral "4." The runways were pocked by craters. Here and there, patches of weeds and brush had rooted on the strips. Along the sides, ranks of brush pressed against the paving, digging fingers underneath, rolling it up like a carpet.

Booker saw other traces of battle. Roofs of Quonset huts, wrecked tanks, mysterious clearings, ammunition revetments, oil drums, and countless little roads that meandered into nowhere, all of it like the glimpse of a lost Atlantis, slowly sinking beneath the waves of vegetation.

The helicopter ride from the airstrips to the beginnings of Bloody Nose Ridge took less than a minute. Suddenly, the whole surface of the island convulsed, heaving up a landscape of limestone pinnacles, crevasses, cliffs, and gorges. No shot had been fired in anger on Peleliu for years, but nature had not restored the looks of Bloody Nose Ridge. Trees nestled in craters and vines dangled over some of the slopes, but Booker had no trouble finding shell marks on the face of the mountain, remnants of steps and paths, numerous cave openings half-blocked by metal doors, like the eyes of a drowsing, unkempt monster.

They hovered over what appeared to be the highest peak. It was riddled with holes. A cruel dentist had gone berserk with a mammoth drill.

The helicopter dipped down. Booker found a concrete-and-stone pillar at the top of Bloody Nose Ridge. The metal letters were rusted but legible.

> LEST
> WE
> FO GET
> THOSE
> WHO
> DIED
> 323
> INFATRY
> U.S. ARMY

"Know what the Palauans say about this place?" Colonel Vincent asked, without pausing for an answer. "According to their version of it all, the wife of a high-ranking Japanese officer was on Peleliu during the fighting. When the outcome was clear, she shaved her hair, donned military clothing, and dug herself in up here, knocking off Americans by the dozen before they finally got here. That's what the Palauans remember."

"How about that?" Booker exclaimed.

"A little ironic note," Colonel Vincent grinned. "I thought you might fit it in somewhere."

Booker doodled away in his notebook. They were at close quarters in the helicopter, so he went out of his way to render the words illegible: Japs Twiff on Hill.

Colonel Vincent enjoyed the first day of the Peleliu operation. He and Booker were up in the helicopter all afternoon, circling the island, dipping down over the airstrips, blitzing Orange Beach, soaring on spontaneous flights among the Rock Islands. Every detail of the slightest interest he made sure Booker saw: the old phosphate mines on Angaur, pitted like the surface of the moon; a Japanese seaplane cave hidden in the Rock Islands. For a while, they chased a pair of rare dugong —sea cows—swimming far outside the barrier reef.

When the light started to fail, the entertainment continued. Colonel Vincent brought the helicopter down on Angaur, where they took supper in the galley at the Coast Guard station.

It was a strange little base, just a couple of low-slung buildings clustered around a red-blinking radio tower, an electric beacon for ships and planes across the Pacific.

Booker enjoyed his meal. The atmosphere inside the galley was relaxed. Soul music alternated with Country and Western, dress rules were unenforced, and Colonel Vincent left him to linger over coffee while he "liaised" with the Coast Guard commander.

Booker was surprised, then, to see two armed guards standing at attention in front of the fence which separated the Coast Guard's alabaster structures from some Palauan shacks. And he was surprised, too, at the hostility of the Palauan youths who clustered around some motorcycles across the way.

"What's the standoff?" he asked when Colonel Vincent returned.

"I see you noticed the problem we're having," the colonel said. "Well, there's no point in hiding anything from the press. The people here are upset and misled. Not just here, all over Palau. All over Micronesia."

"What's got them upset?"

"The movement of marines onto the islands, for one thing."

"What else?"

"Certain rabble-rousing politicians who fear—or claim to fear—that their islands will be taken over again by the military. Peleliu, by the way, is the home of the most virulent. Kintaro. But I wish the problem were confined to him, or to Micronesians."

"Well?"

"You're not going to believe this, Booker. Or maybe *you* will, but it's incredible to *me*. Some of our worst enemies here are our own people, fellow Americans who maintain that, since they're Peace Corps volunteers, their first loyalty is to Micronesia, not to their own country. There are hundreds of them here! Through constant conditioning and propagandizing, they have the Micronesians so wrought up about the military that these people are suspicious of everything we do. We can't ship a can of Spam into these islands after a typhoon without the Peace Corps' starting rumors about new military bases!"

"Interservice rivalry?"

Colonel Vincent stepped in front of Booker and delivered another one of his discomfiting masonic stares.

"It's much more than that. You know, you should do a story about the Peace Corps. It would open a lot of eyes. Draft dodging, marijuana, folk music, slovenly dress—and an utter contempt for every other American presence in these islands."

"Thanks. I'll give it some thought."

"Don't mention it. We're in this together."

It was almost dark by the time the helicopter flew back to Peleliu. Only the heights of Bloody Nose Ridge caught the last orange sunlight. The monument glinted like the top of a skyscraper.

"I've been saving a special surprise for you," Colonel

Vincent said as they approached the Ridge in the 'copter. "Close your eyes."

"What?"

"Close your eyes, really. It's a surprise."

"Oh, come on, Colonel, I'm not playing peekaboo."

"Please! You're going to be amazed."

"Okay, okay. My eyes are closed."

Booker felt the helicopter move into position, maneuvering vertically for just the right angle on whatever wonder Vincent was about to unfold.

"No peeking, now. Don't ruin it for yourself."

"No peeking," Booker assured him. With his eyes closed, he immediately forgot Peleliu. He pictured the workout he was going to give Inez. He felt ready enough now, primed for a real performance. Hell, the way he felt, the two of them could do their dirty deeds on ABC's "Wide World of Sports."

"Okay, open your eyes."

Booker looked down out of the helicopter, down onto Peleliu by night.

"My God!" he exclaimed. "My God, what have you done to this place?!"

The whole island was wrapped in bands of light. Just below the helicopter, the marines had established a searchlight next to the monument. Its beam revolved like the light on top of a police car. It glanced down at the airfield, it reached across the swamps and lowlands to the invasion beaches. And it lit up the stony confusion of Bloody Nose Ridge.

But there was more. Down at the airstrip, a solid line of light, a bright, broad corridor, spanned Peleliu from side to side, marking the distance that Colonel Vincent's searchers had come that day. There were other pockets of light on the beaches. And far down the island, near the Palauan village, searchlights glared against the adjacent mountain. At sea, too, beacons from boats shone in toward the beaches. And at least two other helicopters flashed along the perimeter.

"I've got to hand it to you, Colonel," Booker said. "You're a magician."

"Nobody in those caves is moving anywhere tonight. Even if they tried it, there's more than lights. There are electric sensors all along the perimeter."

"I thought they tried electric warning systems in Viet Nam. And that they flopped."

"That's not true! Pardon me, but I'm a bit of a bug on this equipment, and I don't believe that it's been given a fair shake. In Viet Nam the equipment was dropped from planes, monitored hit-and-miss. The operation was random and scattershot, and so were the results. Here you have a chance to see how formidable, how intimidating this gear can be. Tomorrow there'll be some officers coming down to see this setup. But I couldn't wait. I had to show it to someone tonight."

"I appreciate it. It's a real . . ."

"An exclusive?"

"You said it."

"It's more than that. It's the warfare of the future. I can't let you have pictures of this. I can't even let you close to some of the gear. Yet I'd love to see what a gifted writer could do with this scene. The word picture you'll make of it. The war of the future being tested on a battleground of the past!"

Booker scribbled a word picture in his notebook.

THE SECOND DAY

The next morning, Colonel Vincent had a suggestion. Since the preceding day's tour had given an "overview" of the situation, what Booker needed now was "the nuts and bolts, the nitty-gritty."

Reluctantly—for Booker was a lazy reporter, quite willing to cover the whole search from the command helicopter—the man from *Gotham* donned a T-shirt, chino pants, and sturdy shoes, and climbed into a jeep next to Corporal Billy Dobbs.

"He's to go everywhere he wants, see anything he wants, talk to anybody he comes across," Vincent instructed Dobbs. "No restrictions, except for the special equipment. He can't go backstage."

Colonel Vincent waved the two men away and pivoted back toward his tent. He seemed relieved to be spending the day by himself, Booker thought.

The marines were well beyond the airfield now, outflanking the ridges, moving north on both sides of the island. By the time the jeep caught up with the advancing line, it was nearly ten o'clock. The temperature and humidity on Peleliu were leapfrogging each other into the low nineties.

"Salt tablets?" Dobbs asked. "It's the second best way to get through an operation like this."

"What's the first?"

"Getting about half a load on before breakfast and keep drinking all day."

"What are the chances of doing that?"

"Not good. But Atkinson has some brew at his house."

"Want to drop in on him?"

"You willing?"

"If you are."

"The boss said you go anywhere you want. I'm just the driver."

Bleary-eyed, Atkinson welcomed company. He quickly produced a six-pack of beer from a kitchen which was strewn with empties and smelled of rotting food.

"Have some breakfast," Atkinson said.

He threw some Slim Jim sausages on the table—disagreeable, spoiled-looking cylinders of cured meat and fat.

The demolitions chief was content to sit and drink in silence. Unused to conversation, he preoccupied himself with the Slim Jims. He took the sausages between his thumb and his index finger and, beginning at the top, proceeded to squeeze his way down as if he were milking it, coaxing out a shocking amount of greasy fluid.

"How they doin' down there?" he finally asked Dobbs.

"They've covered most of the level ground. By tomorrow, we should be startin' in on the caves."

"Then this is my last day off," Atkinson said. He reached into a cupboard, rummaged around, and came up with a bottle of V.O. whiskey and some shot glasses. Also, he found some canned potato chips, bottled olives, dried herring, plastic-wrapped cheese and crackers, and two bags of pistachio nuts.

"Party time," he announced. He poured them a shot of whiskey and brought out fresh cans of cold beer.

Booker's stomach started to turn over. It did not want a boilermaker, not at ten o'clock on a steaming tropical morning. But he went ahead and threw the depth charge into his gut.

Outside, the sun blasted blindingly onto the white coral road. In the village, no one stirred. Palauans stayed indoors, dogs and pigs slept in peace under house floors.

"What do you make of this whole search operation?" Booker asked Atkinson.

"How's that?" the demolitions man returned. He was pressing the fat out of two Slim Jims at once now, stroking away.

"You know. Hundreds of marines on foot, on boats, in helicopters. The island lit up at night like a supermarket opening. Isn't that a bit much?"

"A bit much," said Atkinson. "A bit much." It was as if he were hearing the phrase for the first time and wanted to file it away.

"Come on, chief," Booker pressed him. "This is supposed to be about *one* dead man. Even if there are Japanese stragglers around, you're talking about a handful of scared, crazy fifty-year-olds!"

"Somebody's got to do the job," ventured Dobbs. "If it didn't get done right twenty-five years ago, I reckon we'll have to finish it off now before anybody else gets killed."

"Sure, but that makes it a police matter," Booker said. "A job for the local police, not the Marine Corps."

"And you think the local police could do the job?" Atkinson asked.

"Why not?"

"You would send the island constable into those caves to look for armed Japanese? You suppose he could handle it? You suppose you could *make* him go in there?"

"Can't be handled by the cops?"

"Not the cops here. Or the cops they have anyplace I've ever been," Atkinson said. "Those guys need seven shots to kill a dying dog."

"Then you figure Colonel Vincent's going at it the right way, searchlights and helicopters and such?"

"No, I didn't say that," Atkinson replied. "I sure as hell didn't."

"Well, how do you think things should be done here? What's your fix on things, that's what I need to know. You'd be doing me a favor."

"Told you before, I don't owe you no favors. You got my story on tape, and that's all you're gettin'. My momma didn't raise no stupid kids."

"I'm only trying to do a job," Booker protested.

"I'm only tryin' to get through a period of unemployment. Now quit sniffin' around. You want to drink and dine with me, fine. Bullshit, sure. Sports, fishing, your first piece of tail, some girl you boffed was somethin' special, we'll talk. Want another shot?"

"No. Thanks, really, and no hard feelings. But Dobbs and I had better be getting back. Just so I can say that I saw the Marines in action."

"So long, then. See you tomorrow, I guess."

"In the caves?"

"In the caves."

The headache and nausea hit Booker before the jeep jolted out of the village, bumping sickeningly over potholes while the coral glare threatened to squeeze his eyeballs back into his skull.

Heavy, plain-spoken Billy Dobbs led the way into the boondocks. Booker hoped that in the thickets at the base of the mountain, he would find relief from the heat and glare of the flatlands, the woozy, sickening shimmers of heat that rebounded off the island's surface.

But his discomfort was only beginning. The heat in the shade was a muffled, suffocating, greenhouse heat. And, up close to the mountain, the terrain became impossible. Booker slipped and tripped behind Dobbs along a damp trail that made squishing sounds underfoot, winding through places that the sun seldom lit and never dried. Even at the very base of Bloody Nose

Ridge, there were sudden swampy depressions, natural sewers, bogs of mud intersected with broad-leafed taro plants and coils of brown roots.

Colonel Vincent's marines moved slowly through all this, bumping against coral which lacerated their boots, crashing through underbrush whose branches slapped in their faces, wading and cursing through the mud. When he could not see them, Booker could hear them swearing. It was hardly a sneak attack.

At the bottom of the Ridge, Booker and Dobbs sat down next to a resting group of marines. Throwing himself on his back, Booker fought for control of his rebellious stomach and looked up at the mountain they would begin to penetrate tomorrow. Then he decided that doing a little work would take his mind off nausea.

"Flushed out any Japs today?" he asked the marines.

Nobody answered. The word had gotten out. No good came of talking to reporters. No Ernie Pyle chitchat from these recruits.

"No living, breathing Japanese?"

Silence.

"Well, if they're here, they're inside the mountain. Tomorrow you might get some action."

Nothing. Booker's interview was turning into a monologue, and it made him uncomfortable.

"How you fellows feel, getting drafted for Viet Nam and ending up fighting World War II again? Bet you didn't expect to be out hunting Japs."

They hunkered down on their haunches, as quotable as porters on an African safari.

"I'm a reporter, sure, but you can talk to me. I cleared it with Colonel Vincent. He said anybody could talk to me."

"Did he say anybody *had* to talk to you?" asked one of the marines.

He did not look at Booker when he spoke. He was preoccupied by the action around a tiny coral cut on one of his ankles—not with the cut itself, but with the flies which had found the cut, mooring at the tiny oasis of blood. He was counting them.

"Why not talk to me?" asked Booker.

"Ain't no story in me. Who you with, *Stars 'n' Stripes?*"

"*Gotham* magazine. New York."

"Shee-it."

"And *I* think there is a story here."

"Go 'head with your story. Just leave me out of it."

"Mr. Booker! Hey, Mr. Booker!"

It was Billy Dobbs, waving to him from the edge of the boondocks.

"Want to see some Japs?"

"Sure do."

"Down over here."

The marines tensed, ready to move down the slope. Dobbs waved them off.

"No, it's not like that. As you were."

Dobbs led him downhill, away from the Ridge. The trail was steep and muddy, and Booker half walked, half slid down the incline, holding onto roots and branches. Mud covered him from head to toe by the time he reached the bottom.

"It's no big thing, but it's still a find," said Dobbs. He was dirty, too, but he was grinning and pleased with himself, and the sweat that streamed out of his pores seemed a symptom of health, not sickness. He's happy as a pig in shit, Booker thought.

Booker would never have noticed the little hill which attracted Billy Dobbs. It was only a hummock, a pile of coral boulders covered with trees and vines. He would not have noticed where concrete held chunks of coral together, or where rotting beams buttressed the foundations, or where tiny firing apertures peeked out from between the rocks. It was work for a man like Billy Dobbs, and Dobbs was now on top of the hill, brandishing a wooden stake and slamming it down against a piece of metal.

"Come on up here, Mr. Booker, and lend a man a hand," Dobbs shouted.

Together, they wedged the stake under a heavy, rusted plate and, leaning together, lifted against it, prying it loose like a manhole cover.

They wrestled the plate away, and the first daylight —weak daylight, at that—in a quarter of a century filtered into the Japanese fort.

Before they had a chance to peer down through the opening, they heard chaos within, dozens of plops and splashes. Booker jumped back in fright.

Dobbs cautiously shone a flashlight over the opening, followed its downward beam, and broke into laughter.

"Well, I'll be," he said. "Take a look at that."

There was turmoil down below. Dozens of toads, panicked and blinded by the light, thrashed about in six inches of stagnant green water, clumsily bumping into each other, pounding their heads against the concrete walls.

Dobbs was tickled by the agitation he had caused. He could watch it for hours. But he slowly moved the beam of the flashlight around the interior.

The main machine-gun port had been sealed; whether by blasting, bulldozing, or the slow collapse of the wooden bulwarks, it was impossible to say. What little light penetrated was from tiny firing holes high up in the walls.

Whenever the flashlight passed over the watery floor,

the toads started jumping again. Only in one corner, where a pile of wood and earth raised above the boiling water, was there calm. And it was the calm of death.

"There they are, Mr. Booker. In the corner there."

On top of the pile of mud and wood, among canisters of ammunition and rusted mess kits, were the protectors of the fort, now all but merged with the place they had defended. Booker first saw a piece of wet leather gleaming in the light. He followed the bones upward, past a belt, a first-aid kit, and a helmet, until he located a skull on top of the charnel heap. Then, moving to the side, he found some other men. Two or three of them —it was hard to say.

"Musta been a flamethrower cleaned them up," Dobbs said.

He aimed the beam at the wall, and Booker saw that the paint was charred and blistered.

"It's not so bad," Dobbs remarked. "Just like a crypt. With the toads to keep 'em company. You want to climb down there and poke around some, Mr. Booker?"

"No. Definitely not." Booker shuddered, unsure whether the dead bones or the living toads bothered him more. Or the combination of the two.

"Well, then, help me jerry this plate back on top."

"Why?"

Booker stepped back from the opening. A bank of clouds had settled over Peleliu. The first raindrops filtered through the screen of foliage, and of these, a few perfect shots plopped down onto the rottenness at the floor of the fort. Another new experience for the toads.

"Why bust our balls sealing it back up again?" Booker repeated.

Billy Dobbs was embarrassed.

"Now, Mr. Booker, did I help you out a little today? Taking you over to Atkinson's house and guidin' you through the boonies?"

"Sure, Dobbs."

"Well, I showed you this stuff, too, didn't I? I could have kept it to myself, but I wanted to give you material for your story."

"And I appreciate it. But in a minute, it's going to pour."

"That stuff down there is valuable."

"What?"

"The skulls, Mr. Booker, the Jap skulls. I don't want the niggers to find 'em!"

"Why are they so valuable?"

"For trophies, Mr. Booker. Magic tricks, paperweights, conversation pieces, I don't know what all. But I can get twenty-five dollars per. Twenty-five dollars a head."

"Who the hell from?"

"Ah, Mr. Booker . . ."

"From Atkinson?"

Dobbs nodded.

"Okay, Dobbs, we'll close her back up."

"Thanks, Mr. Booker. You won't be sorry."

It was pouring now, but they heaved away with the beam, worked the plate back into position, and covered it with rocks and foliage, leaving the fort as they had found it.

"You want one?" asked Dobbs.

"Want what? A skull?"

"Yeah, I could put one aside for you. Freebie."

"Shit, no. Not in my house."

"You don't get the picture, do you, sir? That's history in there."

That night in camp, there was lively commerce in history, in skulls and sabers, mess kits and medals, and the hope of greater riches the next morning, when the marines would finally enter the underground stronghold of a dead army. There was talk, too, of coral cuts, bites, infections. There was the macabre tale of two marines who had taken shelter from the rain under a tree whose leaves were so venomous that the water washing down on the men's arms and legs and faces raised crops of blisters and burning sores. These were the minor trophies and casualties of the second day.

THE THIRD DAY
Collapsed on his cot, Booker slept through supper and breakfast, awakening on his stomach—bristling, sweating, and nursing an erection he was saving for Inez.

A bad odor penetrated the tent, snuffing out his dream. Booker turned to see Merle Atkinson standing in the doorway, lifting one leg against the tent pole, breaking wind.

"Howdy doody! There's a briefing in Colonel Vincent's tent."

"What about?"

"Oh, caves and Japs and strategy and equipment and the rules of warfare. Jacking off."

"You seem cheerful. Had a drink?"

"Nope."

"Want one?"

"Nope. I never drink before I go into caves. And I don't recommend that you drink, either. Especially since we'll be spelunking on the same team. I don't want to crawl through your piss."

"First, we'll describe the cave system," Colonel Vincent began. "Then we'll analyze our penetration of it."

Stepping to a chart propped up on an easel, holding his pointer like a baton, Colonel Vincent made the cave hunt sound like a sexual act, Booker thought. And it occurred to him that he might use that theme in his story: the discovery of the orifices, the thrust through the tunnels, the men pumping themselves into the mountain.

"What you see here," Colonel Vincent said, "are side views of Bloody Nose Ridge, one from the east, one from the west. Every major tunnel is marked, and groups of you have been assigned to remain outside those openings for the duration. Anything that comes out of the mountain is your responsibility.

"Then, we confront the possibility—the probability—that there are numerous lesser openings, known and unknown to us. For that reason, the surveillance groups will account not only for the openings they guard but for the whole face of the Ridge. If you need more men, or more lights, or more anything, let us know."

Colonel Vincent lifted up one page of the chart and uncovered what was clearly a master plan of the Japanese cave system as it would be seen from overhead if the whole top of the Ridge were lifted. The map showed a half dozen tunnels inside the mountain, all of them connected. Many tunnels appeared to have openings on both sides of the Ridge.

"That, gentlemen, is what we'll be going into, insofar as General Inoue envisioned it."

Vincent looked over at the Japanese general's picture, which was propped up on his desk, and all but nodded at it. It was as if he had unveiled a statue and anticipated a round of applause for the artist, the genius who had sculpted tunnels in limestone.

"What the map does not indicate is as important as what it reveals," the Colonel resumed. "For one thing, it shows nothing of the height or depth of the tunnels. It doesn't tell us which are narrow passageways and which are large chambers. It doesn't tell us where we stand, where we crawl. Also, it tells us nothing of the condition of the caves and tunnels today. But Merle Atkinson can give us some assistance in that regard."

Atkinson shambled awkwardly to the front of the room, a gawky schoolchild reciting in front of class.

"We only just started clearin' out a few caves close to the village. And that's all they were—fortified caves. We hadn't gotten into the major tunnel system yet. All I've done is . . . diddle her a little. Wet my finger some."

A ripple of appreciative laughter went around the room. Booker knew he was not alone in his sexual musings.

"I know that some tunnels are open and others are blocked by boulders, by earth slides, by metal doors, and sometimes by artillery pieces. Once you get inside, you'll find the tunnel is about eight feet high and almost as wide, and the first fifteen feet dip downhill steeply. That, of course, was so they could minimize the effect if somebody shot off into her throat.

"From there on, you play it by ear. You're gonna find a lot of water and mud, a lot of metal and wood and ammunition. You're gonna find some dead men, too. Bats and guano, besides."

"Are there snakes?" someone popped up from the back of the room.

"None poisonous."

"Bugs?"

"Ditto."

"Japs?"

"I don't know." Atkinson shrugged. "But you might

as well watch yourself. You want to remember that you're in a natural limestone formation. The Japs dandied it up some, like you seen on the map. But what nature made is much more complicated. There's gullies, vaults, chambers, probably some underground rivers. Take it from the son of a coal miner—there's lots of ways to die underground."

Next came an inventory of the personnel and equipment that would be entering the caves. There were ten men on a team. The first four men to go down a corridor would all be riflemen, armed and carrying high-powered flashlights. Behind them would come two electricians, who were to string a primitive chain of electric bulbs behind the advancing riflemen. The seventh marine was a radioman. The last three were manual laborers. All the teams were expected to encounter repeated blockages—barricades and debris—in the tunnels. Also, there were rifle teams in reserve, spare crews of diggers who could be called on if the stoppage in the tunnels proved especially formidable. On call, too, were ordnance experts who could handle undetonated bombs, first-aid teams, and some local-hire Palauans who spoke Japanese.

"Sir, if we find some, what are we supposed to do with them?" asked one marine. "Is it war, or what?"

"When you find Japanese?"

"Yes."

"That was going to be my last point," Colonel Vincent said. "No Japanese who is inside the cave system is going to escape. Essentially, they're all our prisoners already, and we should try to treat them as such. The problem, though, is that we might not be able to. Because they don't know we've captured them. Because they're armed, desperate, paranoid fanatics. My instructions, then, are for you to avoid direct engagement when possible. Drive them farther into the caves. When they're finally cornered, maybe we can reason with them."

"Sir?" The same marine spoke again.

"Yes, Michaelson, what is it?"

"Sir, you said that there were Japs down there, right? At least, that the chances were pretty good?"

"Yes, I did."

"And if there are, they probably know about us . . . have seen us creating a cordon around the Ridge, shining lights all over it at night. So we're not going to surprise anybody."

"That's right. This is not a sneak attack. Get to the point."

"Well, this is the point. There's a lot of ammo in the caves, right? Bombs, shells, grenades, so forth?"

"Correct."

"Well, what's to prevent them from killing us all once we're in the caves? Setting off some charges and bringing the whole rockpile down on our heads?"

That stopped Colonel Vincent. And it alarmed the men who sat around the room, who so far had thought of their mission as an expedition, not a bona fide battle.

"Well, Michaelson, there is no guarantee. We may take some casualties. But maybe not. After surviving for twenty-five years, those Japs may want to live a little longer."

"But they haven't been pressed like this before."

"That's enough, Michaelson. This is not a hunting trip. It's a professional military operation. Now let's get on with it."

Atkinson's group had not been given an easy tunnel. They had to climb for twenty minutes before they reached it, clambering over coral boulders and grappling with vines until they reached their entry—a dark, mouthlike opening better than halfway up the side of the Ridge. From where they stood, they could see much of Peleliu, the straits, and nearby Angaur. Farther off, they could see a fleet of clouds heading toward the island.

While they waited for the signal to begin, two marines rigged the storage batteries that would power the string of bulbs they would trail behind them as they entered the caves. The bulbs would do more than light their way into the labyrinth. Spaced every thirty feet, they would enable the men to measure how far they had traveled. The radioman tested his equipment, installed in a backpack.

Finally, a helicopter—Colonel Vincent's command post for the day—appeared overhead, and the leader himself waved them into the mountain.

Dobbs and three other marines led the way. Then Booker, Atkinson, the radioman—a Puerto Rican named Rivera—followed. Last were the electricians and the diggers.

Booker had feared the worst, had seen himself wedging into a hole, squeezing along through a tunnel barely wider than his shoulders. He had pictured the tunnel narrowing, pressing him, had seen himself trapped and caught inside the mountain, unable to advance or reverse, the victim of lethal underground gases, sudden floods, uncontrollable fear. He did not like tight squeezes; he did not want to feel the weight of the mountain upon his shoulders. He did not want to die in a small place.

Entering the tunnel, then, he had to laugh at himself. It was as simple as opening a garage door and stepping inside.

One at a time, they edged past a heavy metal door

which had once slid back and forth to protect the men inside. Now it was knocked off its rollers and rusted.

"Team seven inside Bloody Nose Ridge," Rivera broadcast, more like a sportscaster than a combat radioman.

Behind the door was a massive artillery piece, still trained on the Philippine Sea.

The gun had moved back and forth on tracks once, firing and recoiling so that it could be loaded in safety behind the door. During the battle, the protecting door had saved the gun from American bombardment. After the war, the cave's height and inaccessibility had kept the gun out of the grasp of scrap-metal dealers.

Walking erect, they followed the tracks back into the mountain. As Atkinson had predicted, the tunnel dipped steeply for the first ten feet. Soon they were tracking through mud and water.

Then the tunnel leveled off. The searchlights pointed down a straight, narrow corridor.

The tunnel was easily eight feet high and five feet wide, covered with flaking white paint. Along the roof ran rotted electrical wiring.

"Fifty feet, straightaway," Rivera declared. "No obstacles in view."

"Hold it," Dobbs said.

He was kneeling down over some charred wood.

"I don't know how new this is," he said, looking up at Atkinson.

Stepping to inspect the remains of the campfire, Atkinson kicked a piece of metal. It rattled against the wall. He shone his flashlight over to see what he had booted. A can of Shasta Cola.

"No," Atkinson said. "It's not going to be that easy. Some Palauan kids probably sat out a storm here. Keep movin.' "

Now the light at the opening to the tunnel was almost gone—a tiny porthole onto the daylight world. Slowly and quietly they inched forward. It grew cooler and darker and wetter as they moved along, but not more frightening.

They were two hundred feet into the mountain when they came up against their first obstacle: a solid metal door, firmly in place.

There were latter-day markings on the door, scribblings and scratches, and there was latter-day garbage on the floor, but the door itself was unmoved. Whoever had entered the tunnel since the war had gotten this far, and no farther.

Dobbs stepped forward and took one look at the door. No hinges, no handles, no cracks or corrosion. He ordered Rivera to radio for acetylene torches. The rest of the crew sat back against the tunnel wall and waited.

"They put up a door like that, there must be something on the other side," Booker said to Atkinson.

"More tunnel, maybe," Dobbs said.

"I doubt it," Atkinson replied. "So far, this tunnel has been all man-made, except for that shallow cave out front where the gun is. What's on the other side of the door is probably a natural hollow of some kind, or an underground chamber."

"You think it opens up into a room?" Booker asked.

"Could be," Atkinson said. "We might be coming out on the top or the bottom of it, or in between. And if there's anybody in there, they'll know we're comin'. They'll hear us cutting at the door."

"They could train guns on us," Dobbs said. "Pick us off as we come through. Or lob a grenade."

"So we won't come through," Atkinson said. "Here's the way it's going to be. We'll cut at that door till she's hanging by a cunt hair. We'll turn off our lights—*all* our lights—and kick her in. After that, we watch and wait. If nothing happens, we'll shine our lights into the cave —quick flashes from either side of the door, on and off. Understand?"

"Got it," Dobbs said.

"For a man who doesn't believe in stragglers, you're acting like the cave is loaded," Booker said to Atkinson.

"I take no chances," Atkinson answered. "Not on the Japanese. Not on anybody else."

"Who else do you expect in there? *Germans?*"

Atkinson turned on his haunches and faced Booker. He was not amused.

"Listen, smart ass," he said. "There are a dozen different teams of armed men burrowing into this mountain at different speeds from different directions, feeling their way through shit and darkness. Now what do you think the chances are of someone butting heads along the way?"

They had been in the tunnel almost three hours before they were done cutting. The door which had sealed the tunnel for a quarter of a century now was ready to be pushed backward into whatever lay on the other side.

Holding flashlights, Dobbs and another marine lay on their stomachs at either side of the door. Behind each of them was a rifleman. In between was a marine ready to push the door in with a wooden beam.

For the first time, there was fear in the tunnel. They felt safe from rifle fire, but a grenade tossed into the tunnel would kill—and bury—them all.

Behind them, the string of lights had been extinguished. Rivera's radio was off, too. The whole tunnel had been restored to stillness and darkness.

Dobbs looked back behind him, into the darkness,

then nodded to the man who held the wooden beam.

The marine pressed the beam against the door. It did not budge.

He pressed harder, cursing and slipping, struggling to find a firm footing in the mud.

Booker sensed a movement next to him, felt Atkinson edge past him toward the door.

Atkinson tapped the floundering marine on the shoulder. They both stood up.

"We'll shove at her like a battering ram," he whispered. "Soon as she starts to move, get back down on your gut."

Their first rush clanged against the door; the second effort was louder. The third was unnecessary. When the board reached the doorway, its target was already moving, falling slowly backward into space. The board poked into the air beyond, then dropped to the ground, followed by Atkinson and the marine.

Then came chaos.

Dobbs was supposed to turn on his flashlight first, and so he did. But that was where the planning ended. Instead of reaching out beyond the fallen door, the light danced crazily up and down, because the man who held the light was also moving crazily, swiping at his body, punching at the air, flailing and screaming. So was the other marine, and so, soon, were all of them. Booker felt objects moving past him, brushing his hair, sweeping caressingly over his shoulders. All around him the air was filled with fingers and hands, a current of living things charging out from the inside of the mountain. Booker saw Dobbs swinging his flashlight, saw Dobbs execute a few steps of an Indian war dance, saw Dobbs disappear beyond where the door had been, screaming.

A moment passed before the commotion in the tunnel subsided enough for Booker to hear Atkinson shouting.

"Shut up, settle down! Those are only bats! They won't hurt you. Hold still, and they won't even touch you."

The other marine with a flashlight held the beam out into the empty black space beyond the door, and they could all see that Atkinson was right. Stragglers among the bats were still flying past them, swimming on currents of damp, stale air that blew through the tunnel.

"Where's Dobbs?" Atkinson asked.

"He went inside," Booker answered.

"Can you hear him? DOBBS! HEY, DOBBS!"

The only answer was the flutter of bats escaping down the tunnel.

"Lights off again," Atkinson ordered. "There were bats. But there still could be Japs waiting for us to get over our shit-fits."

Atkinson crawled past Booker toward where the door had been. Flat on the ground, Atkinson snapped on his light, holding it at arm's length from his body and shining it through the doorway. Clearly, the tunnel had come to an end, and Billy Dobbs had disappeared into a larger place than they had seen so far.

From left to right, the beam moved through the air, making contact with nothing more than a few cowardly bats unwilling to risk crossing the pool of light. They swooped back and forth through the light, like a pair of aerialists in an empty circus tent.

At last, Atkinson shone the light down, directly in front of the doorway, and crawled up to it so his eyes could follow the beam downward.

"We're going to need some medics," Atkinson said. "A stretcher. And some rope ladders."

Booker edged forward next to Atkinson. The demolitions chief had been right about their coming into a sizable underground vault. What he had not guessed was that the vault began just behind the door.

Tumbling backward, the door had crashed through the top of a rotten wooden stairway, falling through thirty feet of air, sliding down onto a damp heap of debris, muck, and bat dung at the bottom of the limestone chamber. Billy Dobbs had taken much the same route. He was in the mess about sixty feet below, lying still, face down. His flashlight had rolled six feet away, still shining. Booker remembered advertisements in which nine-lived flashlight batteries came to the rescue of their mortal owners. Now Dobbs's flashlight had eight lives remaining. Its owner, it seemed, had none at all.

Atkinson moved the flashlight back and forth across Dobbs's body, slapping the beam, as if he might somehow revive the man that way.

Then he moved the light around the rest of the chamber. The doorway where they crouched opened near the top. The roof was ten feet above them, dripping stalactites. Booker guessed that it was seventy feet across. From the roof down, the chamber narrowed rapidly. Where Dobbs lay, it was no more than twenty feet across—and an unpleasant twenty feet at that.

Surely Dobbs was not the only human being in that pile of filth, Booker thought. There had to be other men in there somewhere, guns and bones, a quarter of a century farther along that road of decay which Dobbs was only starting on. Little consolation for the amiable Dobbs in the fact that he had fallen on such a pile of trophies.

"You can go back if you want," Atkinson was saying.

"By the time they lift Dobbs outta here, we'll be ready to call it a day."

"He's dead, isn't he?"

"Dead. Or doin' the best damn imitation of it that I've ever seen. His face is straight down. He's got to have his nose full of bat shit. Our first casualty."

"No," Booker corrected him. "Elwell was our first."

"Oh, yeah," Atkinson said. "Let's not forget old Red."

Booker did not wait for them to bring Dobbs out of the cave. He followed the lights back down the tunnel and stepped out into a gray, showery Peleliu afternoon. The marines on guard huddled uncomfortably under heavy raincoats which protected them from the rain but produced the equivalent moisture in sweat. Booker told them that Dobbs had been hurt and made his way back to the camp by himself. He preferred to be rained on.

THE FOURTH DAY

Only Dobbs had perished. But there were other casualties during the first day inside the mountain. One was a marine whose legs had been crushed when a Japanese artillery piece slid backward into a cave. Another had lost his fingers while toying with a Japanese grenade. All of it was accidental.

No one had met any Japanese or come across any signs of recent straggler activity. But what the mountain had failed to produce in living Japs, it more than compensated for with dead. The camp on Orange Beach buzzed with talk of memorabilia. Helmets, canteens, and mess kits were mundane finds. Scraps of bone—carpals, metacarpals, teeth—were devalued after every new discovery. Sabers and bayonets were carefully appraised, and even skulls became subject to exacting scrutiny. An intact skull was valued more than a shattered fragment, of course, but the most esteemed of all was a whole skull with a definite bullet hole in view.

Tales proliferated about what some of the teams had found in the tunnels that day: a whole armory full of rifles and machine guns, an abandoned underground hospital—musty and dripping, bedridden skeletons repining under rotted sheets.

Everyone knew about Merle Atkinson. They spoke of his dealings in souvenirs, the market he made—trading with tourists and Peace Corps volunteers, stocking and restocking caves for the benefit of bereaved Japanese. His home resembled a charnel house, they said. Rows of skulls put up like home-canned vegetables; boots and legs all neatly sorted; whole file cabinets of pictures, letters, diaries. Often, in damp sections of the caves, patches of flesh stubbornly adhered to Japanese bones, cords of muscle and tendon. To cope with these, they said, Atkinson had an oil drum set up in the boondocks to boil the last inconvenient human shreds off his merchandise.

Dobbs's death had prevented Booker's tunnel team from penetrating to where the trophies lay, but a night of gossip on Orange Beach had whetted their appetite. They moved briskly up to the cave that next morning and waited impatiently for the signal to enter the tunnels.

Booker stood next to Atkinson, watching the impatient marines scan the top of the Ridge for the appearance of Colonel Vincent's helicopter.

"They look like they want to go in now," Booker said. "Get a head start."

"Head start on what?" Atkinson asked.

"You know. The stuff."

"What *stuff?*"

"Oh, come on. Early bird gets the worm. You know that. And the birds bring their worms to you. To your little memory shop."

"Mister, what the hell are you tryin' to say to me?"

"They say you've got your own private brand of moonshine going for you on Peleliu, Merle. In fact, you've got your own private still back in the woods."

Atkinson remained on his haunches, sucking pensively on his cigarette. Then he jumped up, and his face was just inches away from Booker's. His eyes were reddish, his breath was sour, and his yellow finger smelled of nicotine. Atkinson placed that finger squarely on Marshall Booker's nose.

"Listen, Mr. Booker. You pick your scabs and I'll pick mine. I didn't ask for you to come bustin' into my life. Don't mess with me on my own ground."

Before Booker could think of an appropriate reply, Colonel Vincent's helicopter dropped out of the sky, and the leader himself waved them into the caves. Atkinson took Booker's elbow and ushered him into the mountain.

Where the tunnel team had inched forward into darkness the day before, they now sauntered down the tunnel, following the string of lights to the blasted-open doorway. The medics who had raised Dobbs's body out of the mud had left rope ladders in place. In less than half an hour, they all stood where Dobbs had fallen.

"Where to now, Mr. Atkinson?" asked Corporal Crabtree, Dobbs's replacement. "You don't suppose this is the end of it?"

"Hell, no," Atkinson replied. "We're still too high up in the mountain. This has got to connect. My guess is that somewhere around here there's an opening for another tunnel that'll take us farther down. We'll have to find it, and we'll probably have to dig our way through it."

Crabtree trained the flashlight around the circumference of the chamber floor. Only ten feet was unobstructed. All the rest was covered with muck.

As soon as the marines determined that there were no tunnels leading off from the clear part of the floor, they began shifting the filth from one side of the floor to the other.

It was disagreeable work. The shovels made slurping, sucking sounds as they squeezed into the muck. They got tangled in wires, banged against pieces of metal. And the very exposure of the insides of the pile released fresh odors of dung and carrion. Even Booker, standing to one side, found himself breaking into a cold sweat that presaged nausea.

Atkinson and Booker lit cigarettes to kill the stench. They leaned against the walls, watching the marines move the pile, the whole exercise the essence of a drill sergeant's cruelty.

They were half done clearing the pile when a shower of rock sprayed down on them from above.

It was followed by the explosion of a single bullet.

"Down, everybody," Atkinson shouted. "Get down! Lights off!"

They fell on their stomachs, dove into the muck.

Far above, even higher than where the door had been, another entrance had suddenly been opened. Out of it, two rifles pointed down at them.

Then a figure fitted itself into the opening.

Crabtree slowly lifted his rifle and took aim.

Booker heard some noises from up above. A hesitation, a clearing of the throat. A voice began to speak, shouting down from above.

In Japanese.

Crabtree's hand tensed on the trigger. He looked over at Atkinson for the go-ahead. But Atkinson pushed Crabtree's rifle down into the mud and stood up.

"Waitaminnit! This is Team Seven down here, and we are not going to fucking surrender! Do you hear me?! This is Merle Atkinson and Team Seven down below. You hear me? Tell whatever shit-for-brains grunt ordered that shot to show his face!"

The stream of Japanese broke off, and the speaker pulled away from the opening. He was replaced by someone who held a flashlight beam down into the hole. The beam found Atkinson, standing up in the spotlight, angry, befouled from head to toe, holding the middle fingers of both hands into the air.

"Sorry, Merle. This is McElroy, Team Ten, up here. You can't be too sure."

"McElroy, turn off that damn searchlight. Take your guns and your megaphone and your interpreter out of the damn tunnel."

"It was only a warning shot, Merle. No harm intended. Find any Japanese yet? Any good stuff?"

"We'll let you know."

Soon afterward, they found what they had been looking for. It was a clogged-up passage, actually a stairway, leading downward.

After an hour spent clearing out another five feet of debris, the stairway was clear, but the concrete steps remained treacherously wet. And there were fallen electric cables which could send a man tripping head over heels. Every twenty steps or so, the stairway widened. This had given the Japanese defenders a place to rest. And room to die.

There were three or four of them at every landing, usually in seated positions, though a few had tumbled face forward, up or down the steps.

"The farther down we go, the better preserved they are," Booker observed.

"Yup," Atkinson answered, flashing his beam over the Japanese.

"More uniform, more flesh," Booker continued. "Even a little patch of hair on some of them. I guess most of them had crew cuts."

"Yup."

Atkinson did not seem pleased at this feast of discoveries. Such vast commodities might glut his market, debasing his inventory. The tunnel should be sealed—as new diamond mines were sealed—to be exploited a bit at a time.

"At this rate, by the time we get down to the basement, we might find some living Japanese after all," Booker suggested.

"Nope," said Atkinson.

"You don't think we'll get any action?"

"Every step we take, I'm surer that all we've got in this mountain is a mother lode of dead Nips. No life and no signs of life. And no action, unless you count Dobbs's belly whopper into a pile of bat shit."

The stairway ended in a tiny area no larger than any of the landings they had passed on their way down. At first glance, the whole passage led nowhere, opened onto nothing.

That did not make sense to Atkinson, or to any of them. Why burrow a stairway hundreds of feet into the ground if it dead-ended in a ten-foot square of damp concrete?

Atkinson must have sniffed something—whether it was novelty, or a new treasure trove, or the death blow to the stragglers theory, Booker could not say. But the demolitions chief was suddenly all over the wall at the bottom of the tunnel, tapping and scraping.

"Gotcha!" Atkinson cried out.

He was scraping his knife against the wall, cutting away at packed mud and rust. When he stood back to rest, the crew admired his handiwork.

It was a round metal plate set inside the wall about a yard above the floor. Atkinson kicked at it, like a hillbilly testing tires on a used car. Then he wheeled around to face the crew.

"If you're willing to work overtime today, I think I can promise you that this will be our last day underground."

"Why's that?" Crabtree asked. "What the hell did you find?"

"It's a crawlway. They used it instead of a doorway so they could control movement through to the other side, and reduce the impact of any explosives."

"What's on the other side?"

"The main Jap headquarters, I'll bet. We're so far down now, it could hardly be anything else. And this crawlway cinches it. This was their last line of defense."

"And they never had to defend it?"

"No, they got mauled up above, the caves got sealed off, or bulldozed, or blasted. Whoever was left behind died on the steps. Starvation. Suffocation. Suicide. Who knows? We get inside here, we can call it quits on Peleliu."

"Let's go!" Crabtree shouted. "Rivera, radio on back to headquarters that we're moving in."

"Now, just a second, men, hold your horses," Atkinson said. "We radio that you're ready to muff-dive into the mountain, you know what'll happen? We'll have Colonel Vincent down here in galoshes, along with the Japanese ambassador, a movie crew, and a helluva lot more reporters than we have to put up with now."

He looked at Booker. He spoke to all of them, but his eyes were on Booker.

"Say we don't radio back," Atkinson resumed. "Say we take this as just another routine step, walk right into the headquarters and look around some. Booker here gets *his* exclusive on what's inside. I get *my* exclusive on what's inside. And everybody gets taken care of."

"Sounds good to me," Booker said.

"Do we have a deal, then? Is everybody in?"

Crabtree hesitated.

"We get a fair shake on the prices?" he asked. "Plus kind of a . . . finder's fee?"

"Everybody's gonna be very happy. I pay you for the stuff, top dollar. I pay you for carrying it out, or for stashing it someplace upstairs. I pay you for keeping your mouths shut."

Crabtree looked at the others. They all seemed pleased.

"Well, then," he concluded, "what are we waiting for?"

Atkinson aped a courtly bow and nodded toward the metal plate. Working their bayonets around the circular rim, they pried it open.

Crabtree shone his flashlight through the crawlway and stuck his head into the hole.

"Looks like you called it, Merle. The crawlway is only about four feet long, and it's open at the other end."

"Could you see anything else?"

"Nope. Just darkness. You smell anything in particular?"

Atkinson placed his head inside the opening and took a whiff.

"Yeah, oil. And stagnant water. I hear a lot of dripping. Hope the merchandise ain't waterlogged."

"One way to find out," Crabtree smiled. "Now who wants to go?"

There were no volunteers.

"We need a skinny guy," Atkinson advised.

That didn't help. Half the crew punched out their guts.

"I guess you could *order* someone in," Atkinson said. "They're all marines."

"I hope it don't come to that!" Crabtree said.

"What we need is a bonus, a little incentive," someone piped up. It was Rivera, the lithe, jive radio man.

"What would that amount to?" Atkinson asked.

"Double share."

"A double share for the disk jockey," Atkinson agreed. "You got it."

Rivera leaned his rifle against the wall, buttoned his shirt sleeves at the cuffs, grabbed a flashlight, and fed himself into the crawlway. His arms disappeared first, then his head and shoulders. He moved easily. Finally his feet lifted up into the pipe.

Atkinson and Booker stood behind, watching Rivera inch away. They saw his feet working against the rounded bottom of the crawlway, his toes pumping him forward a little bit at a time.

Then the toes stopped pumping, about two feet into the tunnel. Later, Booker remembered thinking that Rivera's head must have been through to the other side, that he and his flashlight were exploring what was to be found there.

Both he and Atkinson were paralyzed by what happened next.

They saw Rivera's feet begin to move up and down in place, chopping wildly in the tunnel, turning, flailing, kicking. And from the other side of the wall, a world away, came the muffled sound of Rivera's scream.

Together, they threw themselves against the hole and reached inside, grabbing for Rivera's ankles.

He was still kicking, kicking amazingly fast, like a man having an epileptic fit, pounding against the pipe and screaming.

They both found an ankle and pulled hard, but there was resistance from the other side. His arms are trapped, Booker thought, or maybe he's gotten tangled in something. Why else this tug of war?

Then, as suddenly as it had started, all opposition ceased. The kicking ended.

Atkinson and Booker moved their hands up to Rivera's ankles, to his knees, and the radioman came sliding neatly out, smooth as a drawer in a well-oiled file cabinet.

A couple of marines screamed right away. Booker waited until he had made sure of what he was seeing, that it was true, and then he emptied his breakfast against the wall.

Atkinson sighed, kneeled for a closer inspection of what had befallen Rivera. He alone was unmoved. Pain could move him, not death. He hunkered down and checked Rivera the way a hunter scans a deer's carcass.

Poking his head out of the crawlway, Rivera appeared to have fed himself into a maniac slicer on the other side. The first downward stroke had only clipped his helmet, like a bakery cutter lopping off the heel on a loaf of a bread. That was when the fear had come, when he had kicked and screamed. The second stroke had fallen on the nape of his neck, all but severing his head. The third stroke was gratuitous—a deep chop into the marine's shoulder blades.

"Somebody get on that radio," Atkinson said. "Tell them we have definite hostile contact. Tell them that Rivera's been killed down here. Tell them that I'll meet the colonel up top."

They closed the metal plate and left four marines to stay behind, while the rest of them trundled Rivera up the slippery stairway to the chamber where Dobbs had died. From there, they hoisted him up the rope ladder to the tunnel and brought him out at the mouth of the cave.

Colonel Vincent was waiting for them beside the old Japanese artillery piece. He uncovered the radioman's body, looked him over, then threw the cover back in disgust.

"Their methods haven't changed, have they? The same old style. They damn near chopped his head off! Not a warning sound, either, I'll bet, not a peep out of them!"

"No, sir," Atkinson said. "We figured it was empty in there. We'd walk right in and finish the job."

"You'd walk right in, of course you would," Vincent mimicked. "Right into a vacuum. Well, what do you think now, Atkinson? Am I still a crazy-assed perfesser down from Guam? How about it, Mr. Booker, you taking notes? Am I still the scholarly war lover?"

"Right this minute, you look pretty good, sir," Booker admitted. "There's living people down there after all."

"Yes. There are. Killers in the mountain."

Colonel Vincent looked down at Rivera as if he were reluctant to lose sight of this incontestable proof that his theories had been right—all the old maps, the pictures, the charts, the yellowed photographs of a dead enemy strategist, all finally linking up with a living evil.

" 'We must first resolutely penetrate to the enemy,' " Colonel Vincent intoned, " 'and then we shall display our short swords and slash to the very marrow of his bones!' "

"Beg pardon?" Atkinson asked.

"How's that?" Booker queried simultaneously.

"Just nothing at all, gents," Colonel Vincent smiled. "It's a quotation from General Inoue. From his instructions on the defense of Palau. Armchair, egghead stuff to you guys."

"What do you want to do *now?*" Atkinson asked.

It took some nerve to interrupt the colonel's self-congratulatory monologue.

"What do I want to do now?" Colonel Vincent parodied in a hillbilly accent. "Shucks, let's go on down there and kick a few tires! Let's hoist this theory up a flagpole and see if anybody salutes! Let's throw her in the water and see if she floats! Let's stroke it and see if we get any jism!"

"What do you want to do now?" Atkinson repeated.

"What do I want to do now? What I want to do now, now that we're ready to take this mission seriously, is *get* them. I want to get the Japanese. Is that clear? Could it be more clear? Those antiques, those murderous walking souvenirs, Mr. Atkinson, I want to *get* them!"

"Okay," Atkinson responded. "I think I know how we better do it."

There would have to be several other crawlways leading through to the Japanese headquarters. And there would be several stairways leading down to the crawlways. What Atkinson proposed was simple: Find at least one other crawlway, make a racket which would draw the killers to the first crawlway, then move some men through the second opening in silence and darkness.

Judging from the estimated location of the Japanese headquarters, they guessed that there were two major tunnels which likely led down to the chamber. There was one tunnel high up on the side of the mountain, almost directly over the headquarters. It had not been assigned to a team because it was practically vertical, more like a chimney than a passageway, and it was choked with decayed wooden scaffolding. Colonel Vincent and Atkinson considered lowering someone down into the headquarters but decided against it. The rain of falling wood would alert the Japanese.

The other likely access had gone to Team Four. Impeded by a pile of fallen earth—a recent landslide, by the looks of it—they had been digging away for two days.

"Tell them to keep shoveling," Atkinson decided. "That's the way we're goin' in."

"It'll take time," Colonel Vincent complained. "That tunnel's a mess."

"Well, there is another way. We could drop a bomb through the top, right down the chimney. And forget the whole thing. Just walk away from it."

"No!" said Colonel Vincent. "We'd never know for sure. I want proof."

"I thought you had proof—that guy under the blanket."

"I need something to show on Guam, something Japanese. Drop that bomb, and they'll say I blew up the mountain for the merry hell of it. And some Palauan politician will pop up in front of the United Nations crying about how we despoiled the tourist attraction of the future."

"Well, how about a dose of tear gas?"

It was Booker's suggestion, his first. He had sat all through the planning of the final assault, intimidated by the discovery that Colonel Vincent had been right after all. But the notion of tear gas seemed so obvious, so effective, so humane, he was amazed no one had thought of it.

Atkinson looked away while Colonel Vincent turned to confront the journalist.

"First of all, we haven't got any tear gas. Second, we don't know how it would work in those underground passages—it could backlash against us, blow us off the mountain and leave the Japs free to find a new hiding place. Third—and most important—tear gas is a civilian weapon. And this is war."

He looked as though he would have continued, had Atkinson not interrupted with a question about details. The demolitions chief already knew what Booker had just discovered. Lights and sensors and the other gee-whiz stuff might be fun out in the open, but when it came to confronting the Japs, Colonel Vincent wanted to fight a World War II battle in the bowels of this World War II battlefield.

By nightfall, they were ready. The radio from tunnel four informed them that the marines had shoveled their way through the mud and worked their way down the tunnel. They had stopped at the top of some steps they suspected led down to another crawlway.

This time, there was no keeping Colonel Vincent away from the kill. Dressed in combat fatigues, he drove Atkinson and Booker toward the mountain.

Since the end of the first day, Booker had not been

close to the Ridge after dark. Now he saw that the reconquest of the tunnels had given the place an eerie nighttime beauty. The lights outside the mountain, the lights leading into the tunnel, were like ornaments, embers glowing on a burned-out fire.

The entrance to tunnel four was easily found, marked by piles of wet red clay and broken limestone and concrete, all heaped up outside the mouth of the tunnel, as if the mountain had spewed out its innards.

Colonel Vincent led them down the tunnel, groups of marines stepping aside to let them pass.

When they reached the top of the stairway, Colonel Vincent ordered all lights in the tunnel extinguished.

Five of them started down the stairway in total darkness. Colonel Vincent and Sergeant Ballantine—a brawny combat veteran designated to go through the crawlway first—led the way. Atkinson and Ellert, another tough customer, followed them. And bringing up the rear, more than a little puzzled that they let him trail along at all, was Marshall Booker.

Atkinson had just handed him a piece of paper and a ballpoint pen.

"You'll sign this if you have any hair on your ass," Atkinson said.

It was a release, exempting the United States Government, all its employees, all its agencies from any legal claim resulting from the death or injury of Marshall Booker on Peleliu Island, Palau District, Trust Territory of Pacific Islands.

Even as he signed, Booker was outraged that he had been confronted with the release in a way that left him no choice but to sign. If it had been Colonel Vincent, he would have equivocated. Wouldn't they need all the fighting men they could pack into that tunnel? Wouldn't they prefer not to worry about protecting a civilian? And, shit, hadn't he seen enough tunnels to write a textbook? He'd been down there. Hell, he knew what it was like.

Instead, he was with them in tunnel four, feeling his way down dark, wet, crumbly steps, steadying himself against cool, flaking walls. Where the stairway widened, he knew without looking that there were dead Japanese camped out.

And living Japs waiting at the bottom of the steps, beyond the crawlway.

At the bottom lay a foot of stagnant water. While Atkinson sought the crawlway, the rest of them waited on the steps. This time, Atkinson knew exactly where to look. He scraped away the dirt around the rim and signaled Ellert to help him lift off the metal cover.

Colonel Vincent turned and pointed his flashlight back up the stairway where a group of marines was stationed on a landing sixty feet above. He snapped his flashlight on and off twice—the signal for the marines on the crawlway at the other side to commence noisy preparations for a reentry into the headquarters.

The marines up top relayed the signal. Booker dimly heard the racket begin. It continued for thirty seconds—plenty of time for the killers to return to their chopping block on the other side of the headquarters.

Then, Ellert and Ballantine dove into the crawlway, one with a shotgun, the other carrying a flashlight and a pistol.

Listening carefully, Booker picked up a little sound of splashing as the marines found their footing in the water on the other side. He thought he heard the snap of Ballantine's flashlight switching on. The next sounds were for everyone to hear: a scream and a short burst of gunfire.

Then there was silence.

Atkinson and Booker looked at each other, trading shrugs. Colonel Vincent stood trembling, unable to contain himself. He placed his head at the side of the crawlway and shouted inside.

"What gives? Ellert? Ballantine?"

They did not answer.

"Ellert! Ballantine!"

At last, they heard footsteps splashing toward the crawlway.

They heard someone grunt as he lifted himself into the pipe and shimmied himself toward them.

"Identify yourself, goddammit!"

The crawling stopped.

"It's me, sir, Ellert."

Out popped Ellert's blond mop of hair, his healthy beach-boy face.

"Something wrong out here?" he asked.

"How about in there?" Colonel Vincent burst out.

"You can come in now, sir. It's under control."

"Dead?"

"Yessir, I believe so. It was just like Mr. Atkinson said it would be. When we turned on the light, he was standing over against the wall with a knife in his hands, waiting for someone to come crawling through. I switched on the beam, and we had him like a blinded deer. He screamed, but I doubt he ever focused in on us. Ballantine about shot him in half."

"There was *one* man?" Colonel Vincent asked. "Only *one?*"

"Yessir, just one. He's a big mother, too, for a Jap. I wouldn't want to go hand-to-hand with him."

The Japanese headquarters was one large room, floored with concrete and roofed by a jagged limestone dome. At the center, islands in a lake of putrid, oily water, were workbenches and tables, radio and electrical equipment. At the edge, where the roof sloped down to the floor, cots and desks and filing cabinets were fitted. There were treasures here for Atkinson—stacks of weapons, whole armories shelved into the wall like wine bottles, desks covered with charts, manuals mulching into pulp. And around the circumference, nestled into little crevices and crannies, were patches of wet cloth and rotten leather, glints of bone from places where the Japanese had cached themselves to die.

Water dripped down constantly, heavy plunking drops, quick little pitter-patter streams, steady gullies of sweat coursing off the walls.

"Well," Ballantine said, chuckling, "this is it, all right, sir. Welcome to the Führerbunker."

"Quiet!" barked Colonel Vincent. "Where's the man you killed?"

"Right over here, sir. I'm sorry there weren't more."

They splashed and tripped across the floor of the headquarters, squeezing between collapsed tables, tangling in the fallen wiring. They neared the place where Ellert stood against the far wall, assisting the first member of the other team through the crawlway.

"Get back!" Colonel Vincent shouted when he saw what Ellert was doing.

"Sir?"

"Get that man back. I don't want anybody else in this cave yet. Get him right back into the pipe."

A puffing red-faced marine, half out of the crawlway, looked up at Ellert, shrugged, then retracted into the pipe.

"Tell them to close the metal plate on the other side," Colonel Vincent said. "I want it sealed up."

Ellert whispered a command through the pipe, and they heard some clanking from the other side.

"Okay," Colonel Vincent said, "where is he?"

"You walked right past him," Ellert said. "He rolled down across the floor."

Vincent had missed the corpse. The man was flat on his stomach in six inches of water, his head resting against the blades of a fan that had fallen off the ceiling.

But Atkinson had been more alert. Atkinson did not miss his prey. Atkinson was kneeling beside the dead man, as he had kneeled beside other dead men, appraising the death. With Rivera, he had been clinical, but there was something about this dead Japanese that inflamed him. Waiting for Colonel Vincent to approach, he was red-faced and angry, muscles pumping at the corner of his jaws and a steady whisper of obscenities hissing from between clenched teeth like steam escaping under pressure from a pipe.

"I guess we got our man," Colonel Vincent said.

"Oh, you sure enough did get him," Atkinson said. "Colonel, is this the first Japanese straggler you've ever eyeballed?"

"Why, yes. Yes, he is. Shall we have a look at him?"

"Certainly, sir. After all this work, we deserve a gander. Where do we begin?"

He slapped the dead man on his rump, a butcher sizing up a haunch of beef.

"He's a hefty bastard, isn't he, Colonel? For a ghostly straggler subsisting on snails and bats for twenty-five years."

Atkinson raised the dead man's ankle.

"Found hisself some tough shoes, too, in his own size. Not like those rubber boots his buddies wore. Pants and shirts, too. Resourceful bugger. Well, they are a clever race of people, I hear, and I sure don't want to underestimate them. We made that mistake once before, didn't we?"

He shone his flashlight on the back of the straggler's head.

"Hey, hey, hey! Nice head of hair on this Jap, not a streak of gray. Greased down, too."

He ran his fingers through the man's hair, then raised them to his nose.

"Pomade! Next thing we know, we'll find he got a movie projector and a stash of porn down here."

Atkinson stood and turned over the man's head with his foot.

The dead man had coarse features—a porcine face, wide nostrils, chins to spare. His skin was almost as black as his hair.

"Damn dark for a Jap, isn't he, Colonel? Why, this sonofabitch would leave a thumbprint on coal!"

Now Atkinson faced Colonel Vincent, who seemed uncomfortable, even sick.

"Colonel, he's your baby. You can run blood tests, take fingernail parings and urine specimens, autopsy all week. But you're not gonna turn him into a Jap. He's a Palauan. Maybe he's a drunk, or a crazy. Maybe he did kill Elwell. I don't give a shit. But he's not Japanese. He's not a member of your phantom fucking army!"

Atkinson strode away, cursing. The colonel remained over the body, an image of mourning.

"There are no Japanese on Peleliu, Colonel. I know it, and you know it. They all went home."

"How you makin' out down there, old buddy?"

Beckman's voice insinuated itself through seven hundred miles of static, to the communications tent on Orange Beach.

"I'm a proctologist," Booker replied, "looking up the asshole of the world."

"Hunting's no good?"

"Colonel Vincent bagged himself a Palauan. Nobody knows what the hell he was doing down in the caves. Or, for that matter, just who he is."

"Did the Palauan kill Elwell?"

"Who knows? Not alone, he didn't. But he probably chopped up a marine who came crawling into his hideout."

"So what's Vincent up to?"

"He's broken-hearted, ever since he failed to find the Imperial Army. I hear there's a few caves at the north end they're going to check next. I don't think his heart's in it anymore."

"I sure hope he stays out of *our* hair for a while. What are your plans?"

"I'm leaving Peleliu tomorrow. Atkinson's giving me a ride on his boat. Then, it's a question of catching a flight out of Koror."

"That might take a couple days. In Koror, check in with the distad guy I mentioned to you. Tom Dunbar. I'll radio him and have him meet your boat. VIP treatment."

"What does VIP treatment amount to in Koror?"

"If it's tomorrow night, it'll probably mean a front-row seat at the high school graduation. And you'd better go. There figure to be some fireworks."

"Are you kidding? God doesn't intend Marshall Booker to cover high school commencements."

"I'm serious. This local character, Kintaro, is speaking. He's more than likely to pop off about the Americans. Catch his act."

"Okay. But I want to get out of here."

"When you do get back to Guam, there'll be something nice waiting for you."

"What's that?"

"Inez, man. I saw her the other night on the dance floor of the Fujita, looking bitching. Had one of those disarming white dresses on. Simple, like a nurse's uniform, but it really shows what the woman is like."

"Don't tease me, Beckman. I'll pole vault to Guam!"

"No, get this, she wasn't alone, I'm not going to ask you to believe that. But she did make a point of coming over and asking me when you'd be landing on her island again. She didn't have to do that."

"No, I guess not."

"Know what? I think she likes you."

"Despite that first date?"

"Oh, she understands. You'll see."

There are a lot of insecure reporters around. Some of the very best are the most nervous.

They arrive in new places, traveling on other people's money. They check into hotel rooms and make phone calls, leaving messages for people they don't know. They read the visitors' guides, what's doing in town, get to know the room-service menus. They watch television and jiggle their list of questions, inventories of professional curiosity—worked up for the occasion. They get around a little, arriving early for interviews, filling their notebooks with scribbles. A possible lead paragraph brightens them up. They pounce on a lively quote. In the local newspaper morgue, they come across an earlier story on their assignment and sigh in relief: Someone has been there before. Confidence builds.

At night, they comb through their notes, underlining the bright spots, separating what they have gotten from what they need to get. They reread clips. They frame new lists of questions, more pointed, more specialized. And they despair. Their notes are trash—odds and ends, hackneyed descriptions, recycled quotes; moldy anecdotes—all surrounding an initial cliché of a story idea. They kill their story. They make long-distance phone calls, wondering what the hell they are doing where they are. And they persuade themselves that enormous changes, vast coups are going on back at the office—transfers, resignations, power plays. Having schemed to escape, they now plot to return. This, they tell themselves, is the time they come back with nothing. Every by-line, every past accomplishment has been stored up against the morning when they breeze into the office and announce that there was no story out there. They rehearse the scene: "Nothing there, boss. I don't mind skating on thin ice, but only Jesus could walk on water."

Back to work, bothering people, getting put off, wearing out their welcome. Too soon after breakfast, they have a heavy lunch with someone they do not like. At night, they buy drinks for informants. After a week of deaths and rebirths, they leave town with something which might or might not run. They depart as worried as when they came.

The night before leaving Peleliu, Marshall Booker worried not at all.

There were a dozen different stories he could write out of this assignment, out of any assignment. Booker was the rare reporter who could turn in a piece which answered questions or asked them. He could get a story or, if he struck out, could write an entertaining piece on the funny ways in which he had failed to get the job done.

Gotham had already gotten full measure from him.

Indeed, he had come as perilously close to "overkill" in his reporting here as on any job in years. After four days with Colonel Vincent, he had a lively cast of characters —Vincent himself, a scholar entangled in visions of old wars; Atkinson, the Snopesian bone trader; Billy Dobbs and Rivera perishing in that charnel heap of a mountain. And there was Peleliu itself, the scarred ridges and subtle tunnels, beaches and airstrips, unexploited, unloved, fresh literary territory.

That left Elwell and the question of who killed him. Booker knew he could take liberties here, evoking all the possibilities and eliminating none. Nobody was going to sue.

He began packing. He hitched up his trousers, feeling a pleasant heft below. He was going to be well taken care of on Guam, drinking with Beckman and playing extra-inning night games with Inez. Well taken care of.

PART TWO

FIVE
A NIGHT IN KOROR

I

God, thought Thomas Dunbar, how that man talks!

The High Commissioner of the Trust Territory of Pacific Islands, James Patton Hoyle, was addressing the graduates of William Halsey High School, Koror, and Dunbar was bored. After twenty years of ceremonies, the speeches all sounded the same to him. Even more, the high commissioners—there had been eight of them, so far—began looking alike, smelling of exile and patronage and the convenient kick upstairs.

While the "Highcom" carried on about democracy in the Pacific, the goals of the Trusteeship, the unique partnership between America and Micronesia, distad Dunbar scanned the grounds of Admiral Halsey High.

There was not much to see. The classrooms were tin-roofed hotboxes, periodically ravaged by typhoons which sent sheets of metal roofing slicing through the air like razor blades. There were half a dozen decrepit Quonsets, dormitories for students from remote villages. Underfoot, even, were relics of the Japanese era—steps, bullet-pocked foundations, run-over gardens. Already, the Palauans were clamoring for a modern new school "just as good as Guam." All this mass of war surplus and peacetime improvisation would be bulldozed into the mangroves. The Palauans would have their new school. And they would not name it after Bull Halsey.

The graduates fidgeted throughout the Highcom's speech. The distad saw feet tracing, erasing, retracing patterns in the dust, as if unfamiliar leather shoes were a new writing implement. Commencement programs were being folded into fans, ripped into confetti.

They were not a sitting-still people, the Palauans. Dunbar looked at the boys, dressed in white shirts and black slacks, hair greased down with pomade. Tough and aggressive, they were the Jews, the Ibos, of the Pacific. Elbowing aside competitors from other districts, the Palauans always won a disproportionate share of government scholarships. Even the dullest boy plotted his departure for Guam, where he could enlist in the United States Army, returning to Palau in uniform with wealth and honor. And there were the girls, dressed in white blouses and black skirts, deceptively like convent girls. Time was when Dunbar had thought of every graduating class as a fresh harvest of temptations, the award of a diploma nothing more than a sexual hunting license.

Maybe the Palauans would name their new high school after Francisco Kintaro, the featured speaker of the day. Palauans were notoriously contentious and quarrelsome, but when it came to dealing with outsiders, they usually pulled together. And the man who pulled them together these days—who threatened to liberate the same islands which Halsey had conquered—was Kintaro.

Dunbar looked down the dais to where Kintaro sat waiting for the high commissioner to finish. Short, dark, heavyset, Kintaro was an anomaly to his fellow Palauans, a quirky, unpredictable expatriate. Just returned from college in Hawaii, Kintaro trailed signs of his Americanization there: a taste for scotch, for steak, for *Time* magazine. He was the only Micronesian Tom Dunbar had ever seen willingly eat cheese.

If anything, Kintaro seemed bored with the Palau he had returned to—the subsistence economy, the caretaker government, the slow circular life of villages and islands.

But it was more complicated than this, and the Palauans who supported him knew it. Boredom and anger, loathing and self-loathing were tangled in Kintaro with undisputed ability: He was a leader, not because Palauans loved him, but because they thought he could handle Americans.

For a long time—longer than usual, longer than necessary—Kintaro stood in silence at the speaker's platform, as if his very arrival there were an event worth noting.

The crowd quieted down remarkably. Even after they had hushed, Kintaro kept standing, until the distad wondered if he was going to begin at all.

Kintaro was a plump, awkward figure in white saddle shoes, dark baggy slacks, and a white synthetic-material shirt with short sleeves and a plastic "pocket saver" holding a pair of expensive ballpoints.

His voice, when it finally came, was strained and shrill, searching up and down for the right pitch. But Kintaro did one thing with his voice that was extraordinary.

He was speaking first in Palauan.

The sentences came tumbling out, the guttural, nasal sounds of what the district administrator had always thought more a parody of a language than a language itself, and which his marriage to a Palauan woman had reduced—not increased—his need to master.

The effect on the students and their parents was immediate and startling. Heads popped up, bodies bounced out of slouches and sat erect, girls held each other's hands to contain an unprecedented excitement.

On the platform, too, there was a reaction, a chain reaction moving down the Americans like a row of toppling dominoes: the high commissioner casting a sharp look at the deputy high commissioner, and the deputy —adroitly skipping the Seventh Day Adventist missionary who was there to deliver the benediction—turning to Tom Dunbar. Dunbar shrugged.

"When we speak, we speak to be understood," Kintaro said.

He had turned around. Leaning against the podium, he faced the Americans and spoke in English. But it seemed to Dunbar that the words in English were more for the benefit of the Palauans than for the Americans, as if Kintaro were a tour guide who had paused in front of a caged specimen with whom he could communicate in an alien tongue.

"So that I may be fully understood, I'm giving my speech first in Palauan, then in English. With your permission. Likewise, copies of my text are being released in the other districts of the Trust Territory, translated into the local languages, and accompanied by remarks from the leaders of those districts."

With a curt nod, he turned back to the audience and started again in Palauan.

"I am taking an autobiographical approach," Kintaro finally told the Americans. "Recalling how the sight of American planes over our islands, strafing our villages, was the first sight we had of the people who would become our 'administering authority.' I am telling them that a bullet in my foot—a bullet intended for some Japanese, no doubt—has always reminded me of how this Trusteeship began, and that the lesson I carry with me, with every step I take, is a lesson all Micronesians must learn. We cannot forget that the Americans did not come to liberate us from the Japanese, but to conquer these islands for their own use, and to keep them for their own purposes."

Again, he turned his back. It was turning into a peculiar performance. Before the crowd, Kintaro was intense and fervid, but when he faced the Americans, his manner grew relaxed and ironical. He seemed to be commenting on his own performance, apologizing for its lack of subtlety. The audience, of course, noticed none of this. They were too delighted at knowing ahead of time what Kintaro was going to say to the Americans.

"Has the American mission in these islands been to lead us to self-government—as the Trusteeship Agreement specifies? Or to keep the islands for renewed strategic use in future wars—as the Trusteeship Agreement *also* specifies? What is the true face of our administering authority? Would America create a new democracy in the Pacific? Or another garrison state, like Guam?"

Kintaro turned to the crowd. Dunbar could barely make out their faces in the darkening schoolyard, but he sensed their excitement. Were they responding to Kintaro's message? Or were they only enjoying his pyrotechnics?

"We could not ask these questions in the past. We could not ask them in time to save our burned villages, ruined roads and causeways, poisoned reefs, to save ourselves from the destruction of the last war. We could not ask in time to save Bikini and Eniwetok from nuclear tests. We would not have known how to frame our words, our doubts, our hopes. We would have waited, passive and trusting, for the next war, the next trusteeship, the next administering authority to wash over our islands, just as the Germans followed the Spanish, and the Americans followed the Japanese!"

Again, Kintaro turned to the audience and took up his speech in Palauan. Now, his voice had found its right level, and the distad could practically see the sentences curling and lashing into the air above the audience, exciting the boys, inflaming the girls.

Suddenly, Dunbar detected something familiar in Kintaro's Palauan. He heard him use an English-sounding word, and heard him use it again, and again—one familiar word bobbing around in a maelstrom of Palauan, like bits of wreckage off a sunken ship.

The word was Elwell. Elwell. Elwell.

"A man named Elwell died on Peleliu a few days ago," Kintaro finally translated. "This Elwell was a hero, they tell us, a hero of the great battle on Peleliu. A great American marine. But to us, he is no hero! When Elwell fought here and won, our islands were lost to us. When Elwell returned and died, we lost Peleliu again! There are marines on Peleliu this minute, seizing our land, restricting our liberty, preparing for a new war!"

For the last time, Kintaro turned back toward the audience. This time, when he spoke, there were shouts from the edge of the schoolyard, applause and cheers breaking out among the graduates.

When Kintaro pivoted to face the Americans, there was even more cheering; it increased as he moved across the platform to face the high commissioner. To the audience, it must have seemed that he was daring the Americans to strike back at him.

"Elwell was the last! There must be no more Elwells passing through our islands, changing our lives without our consent. No more Elwells, to win or lose our islands, for our islands belong to us, and the time has come for us to claim them."

Kintaro mopped at the perspiration that escaped between the folds of his chin. Puddles of sweat glued his shirt to his body.

"What we ask," he continued, "is no more than what Americans ask for themselves—the control of our lands, our government, our destiny. We are going to find out if America intends to keep its promises to us."

Kintaro glanced back at the schoolyard, at the disordered rows of wooden chairs and torn programs. A few spectators had left, but around the front of the wooden platform, dozens of graduates remained, a cadre of fanatics. Tom Dunbar had known most of them since they were children. His own children had grown up with them, attended the same schools. That did not matter now. When he sought their eyes, they denied him recognition.

The distad decided he needed a drink.

II

The Darling Bar was no different from the seventeen other bars which served the seven thousand residents of Koror. Like the Boom Boom Room, the Cave Inn, the Blue Gardenia, the Texas Saloon, and the 69-Feeling Bar (so named after a bartop entertainment improvised by a barmaid and Coast Guardsman), the Darling Bar had a metal roof, concrete floors, plywood bar, rickety wooden tables covered by sticky oilcloth, Kirin and Asahi calendars on the wall, and a jukebox in the corner —a crazy melding of mournful Japanese love songs, outdated rock-and-roll, and lachrymose Country and

Western ballads about love, pain, and divorce.

On an empty night, rain drumming on the roof, barmaid asleep over a comic book, a Palau bar could seem like the end of the world. But there were nights—and this night, after the graduation ceremonies, might be one of them—when magic happened. There were payday Fridays—tropical *Walpurgisnachts*—when sleepy-eyed government clerks exploded on manic sprees, when sardonic barmaids sloshed drinks over polite Japanese tourists, when barnstorming Micronesian politicians panted after puzzled Peace Corps girls. On nights like these—roiling stews of smoke and lust, polyglot fighting and screwing—Tom Dunbar did not count the beers he drank or the shots that followed. Beer can in hand, he danced foolishly, pawed rumps and fondled breasts, sat back at tables and howled. On such nights, the distad stayed until nearly dawn, when a Jesuit priest rose to a microphone as if to deliver a benediction and instead offered a heart-wrenching treatment of "Unchained Melody," all the night's sweating combinations swaying, leaning, rubbing up in front of him—his flock of sinners. Nights like this, Dunbar was moved at being in this bar, on this island, so moved that he felt close to tears. No place in the world he would rather be.

Angie was working the bar when Dunbar came in. She was in her thirties now, but the district administrator could still detect—in her grin, in the body English she put into her greeting, in the privileged way she extorted his quarters for the jukebox—the young girl who had torpedoed his American marriage fifteen years before. Three children, a pair of common-law husbands, and a long line of lovers had intervened since then. Angie had not been very particular. Her body had filled and slackened, swelled and sagged too often, but she still stirred him. In the idiom of Palau, Angie was his "it was."

As soon as he sat at the bar, Angie produced a plate covered with white fillets of raw fish, fresh and meaty and cut to bite size. Doused in lemon juice and soya, dipped in hot Japanese mustard, the sashimi made a perfect complement to beer.

Angie sidled down the bar to wait on other customers. The distad watched her walk away. She had gotten a little too heavy for the flowered dresses with slit slides, but she was enough like the younger Angie to make him twinge. It was.

Nearby sat a tableful of Peace Corps volunteers. Without hearing a word from his fellow Americans, Dunbar knew what they would be discussing—the inefficiency and duplicity of his administration, the cynical villainy of the United States military, the corruption and exploitation of Palauan culture. Their themes were constant.

"THE PEACE CORPS IS GOING TO PARADISE."

Dunbar's relatives had sent him the recruiting brochure. A few months later came the Peace Corps itself. He had met them at the airport, three dozen newcomers flushed with rhetoric about "host country counterparts," "agents of change," and "crosscultural experience."

Again and again, however, they had fallen victims to native pragmatism. For the go-getting Palauans were not much impressed by the new breed of Americans who protected local culture, cared about the environment, struggled with the language, and vowed voluntary poverty.

Dunbar had joined in the paeans of welcome, the proclamations of tripartite partnership among the

Trust Territory government, the Peace Corps, and the Micronesians. And he had quietly watched the Peace Corps struggle to preserve what the Palauans were most anxious to exploit. The volunteers stumbled through Palauan while Palauans inched their way through *Time;* the Peace Corps warned about military bases while Palauan youths rushed to Guam to enlist; the Peace Corps forbade volunteers the use of any vehicle more noxious than a bicycle, while Palauans dreamed of Datsuns and Hondas; the Peace Corps protected the fragile ecology of the islands, the life-giving reefs, the forested islets, immaculate beaches, while Palauans would have bulldozed every island, paved every beach, murdered every last turtle and sea cow for the sake of fast roads, new cars, and a ticket to Honolulu.

A bargirl had put it well one night down the road at the Boom Boom Room.

"Palauan people respect the Peace Corps," she said, "but not very much."

Dunbar's wife had put it better still.

"The Coast Guard leaves babies behind. The Peace Corps leaves babies behind and worries about it."

The distad laughed quietly and dipped another slice of sashimi into the hot sauce.

"Raw, I say, is that *raw* fish you're eating?"

Marshall Booker, too, was making a night of it. He had introduced himself to the distad just before the commencement ceremonies. The journalist was dressed in an immaculate blue shirt and crisp white ducks circled by a multicolored cloth belt. He smelled of cologne and after-shave lotion and success on islands larger than Koror.

Dunbar passed him the plate of sashimi. Booker recoiled in mock horror.

"I wouldn't use that stuff for bait," he said. "I'm a country boy. Meat and potatoes."

"This is fish and rice country. Did you make your reservations out of here?"

"All squared away. Tomorrow afternoon I'll be in Guam. And tomorrow night . . . look out!"

"What?"

"Tomorrow night, Marshall Booker is going to be a bad boy. And believe me, after a week on Peleliu, it's all I can do to hold on. That barmaid's nice stuff."

"Want to meet her?"

Booker cast a long look down the bar, where Angie was pouring a trayful of rum and cokes, laughing as she worked, and doing a little step in time with the music.

"She's not bad," Booker said. "Nothing in short supply."

"She could swallow you and spit you out."

Booker tore himself away from the contemplation of Angie. He was one day away from Inez, the focus of a full week of increasingly lively fantasy. He wanted to be ready for her.

"No, thanks," he said reluctantly. "I'm promised to another."

"Your choice," said the distad. "I'll buy us a drink."

Dunbar signaled to Angie. As she walked toward them, a signal passed between the distad and the barmaid, a message transmitted in some ancient body semaphore. When Angie served their drinks, she lingered at their end of the bar, shouting to one of her sisters to look after business elsewhere. With that, she perched on a stool directly opposite Marshall Booker and slowly measured him up and down with her eyes. The survey seemed to please her. Leaning forward, she whiffed Booker's after-shave lotion, filling her lungs with the scent.

Booker felt Angie take his hand and place it flat against the bar.

"What, she's going to read my fortune?"

"In a manner of speaking," Dunbar replied.

But no, Angie was not interested in Booker's lifeline; she sought a much shorter span. She had taken his middle finger and bent it forward across his palm, so that the tip nearly reached his wrist. Then, marking the spot on the wrist with one of her own fingers, she extended Booker's finger to its previous position. Between where Booker's finger had rested on his wrist and where it now pointed into space, there lay a good eight inches.

Angie plunged into a stream of delighted Palauan, marveling at the length.

"What the hell goes on here?" Booker asked.

"It's a little trick some of the girls picked up."

"What is it?"

"It's very simple. The theory is that the distance between where your finger reached on your wrist and where it reaches fully extended represents the length of your tool."

Booker looked down in astonishment. Before he could move, Angie again seized his hand and repeated the ritual of measurement. Confirmation of her first estimate heightened her enthusiasm. She took one finger of her own and slowly drew it the whole length she had measured, tickling Booker's palm along the way.

"How long you'll stay in Koror?" she asked Booker.

"I'm leaving for Guam tomorrow," the journalist replied.

"So, tonight."

Booker fought to control himself, mourning that he did not have a day or two between a night with Angie and the next day's reunion with Inez. But one look at the barmaid told him that a night with this outrageous Angie would ruin his ability to entertain Inez.

With a last forward lean, pressing up against the journalist's perspiring chest, Angie dropped Booker's hand and hurried down the bar.

"Wow," was all Booker could say.

"That's Angie," the distad said.

"She comes on a little strong."

"She does. I believe you'd do well to drop by a little before closing time."

"When does this place close?"

"Supposedly, at 2 A.M. That's because of the curfew I imposed to control the drinking problem here. Sometimes they stay inside behind the doors and drink awhile longer, if everyone's in a good mood. Usually, on a payday Friday, someone ends up buying a case of beer, and a bunch of 'em go out to one of the old Japanese seaplane ramps. They sit around singing and drinking till dawn."

"I can't drink till two in the morning!"

"Can I drop you someplace?"

Booker never had a chance to answer, never even had a chance to think. From behind, someone—someone strong—pulled him off the barstool and spun him around.

Marshall Booker found himself at the center of the room. The Darling Bar was packed now with drinkers at every table and against the walls. There were elite, dressy Palauans in aloha shirts, grimy beer drinkers in T-shirts, tattooed old-timers. There were Okinawan fishermen collapsed on tables, American government workers, Peace Corps volunteers. Outside, Booker glimpsed what was already a familiar tableau: tough-looking youths in motorcycle helmets leaning against the doorway, old women and grinning children peeking through the screens. But all that was just a backdrop. In the foreground, inches away, was Angie. And Angie wanted to dance.

Booker heard a Palauen woman singing in a corner of the room, an eerie, nasal falsetto, followed by handclaps.

Gesturing that he should follow her lead, Angie began a slow, pelvic rotation, moving from side to side, like a hula, but—unlike anything ever seen in Hawaii—she also moved slowly downward, as if she were seating herself on, and rotating upon, an infinitely pleasurable perch. Booker stood across from her. He was petrified.

"Go join in," Dunbar shouted from behind him. "It's the Palauan welcoming dance!"

What Angie was doing looked a little like a twist, a very slow twist, and that is what Booker proceeded to imitate. As soon as he began to move, a hoot of derisive laughter sounded from a corner of the room. But Angie nodded; Booker's moves seemed to please her. She indicated that he ought to move up and down as well, joining her in a swiveling, hunkering motion a few inches above the floor.

Booker's knees bent as if they were on hinges. He headed down. It was all he could do to combine the pelvic motion, side to side, with his floorward crouch. Memories of Melina Mercouri in *Never on Sunday:* he extended his hands, clicking his fingers. That improvisation drew another round of hoots from the audience and an agreeable smile from Angie.

The music built toward a crescendo. Marshall Booker raced after the beat. Angie was still far below him, sweeping the floor with her ass, arms outstretched, and eyes facing straight ahead, riveted, it seemed, at the level of Booker's genitals. He twisted his way down to her, swaying and dipping. More gleeful hoots: the welcoming dance was also an initiation in humiliation. The crowning embarrassment came suddenly. All at once, Booker fell backward on his ass and elbows. The music stopped, the Darling Bar exploded into applause and laughter, and Angie was standing over him, moving in a little ecstasy of victory.

By the time Booker rejoined the distad at the bar, the jukebox was grinding again: Creedence Clearwater Revival singing "Proud Mary." Angie had vanished.

"You earned a drink," the distad said.

"Did you say that was a *welcoming* dance?"

"Don't worry about the fall," said Dunbar. "Palauans like to see a white man make a fool of himself."

"Looks like the whole island comes out drinking."

"There's no television yet," the distad said. "There is on Saipan. One station with five-day-old newscasts and reruns. The whole island sits home watching 'Hawaii Five-O.' But not here. Not yet."

"It's going to change, though. This whole crazy-ass scene. You know that."

"I do."

"For the worse."

"Probably," the distad said. "I hope I retire before it happens."

"Where to?"

"Oh, here. I have some land—or my wife does—on Arakebesan Island."

"Staying here for your wife's sake?"

"And my own. I like it here."

"Stay here, and you won't escape the changes. Tourist hotels for the Japs. Planeloads of soldiers on R 'n' R. Kentucky Fried Chicken. Look out, baby. Somebody's got to fill the vacuum."

"So what am I supposed to do?" the distad asked. He sounded bitter, and he was getting drunk. "Run away?

Run away to a tropical island? I already live on one. Oh, I know it's fucked, don't get me wrong. I know. Four hotels are already on the drawing boards, all financed by the same Japanese interests who've had every store in Koror in hock for five years. The number of cars on Koror is already in the thousands—which is remarkable, considering we have twenty miles of the world's shittiest roads. And look at Koror itself—overcrowded already, and more people coming in from outer islands all the time, forgetting how to farm, how to fish, how to live on their own lands. Anything for a dollar-twenty-five-an-hour job in a white shirt in my piss-poor government. Then you have the bright boys coming here from college. Political science majors, lawyers, economists. What are they supposed to do? What am I supposed to do with them?"

"People like Kintaro?"

The distad nodded.

"A thousand Kintaros. A nation of poly sci majors."

"What do they want? Independence from Uncle Sam? Or more money?"

"Both, if they can get it. They go independent, and we pay for it. Lower the flag and apply for foreign aid. Oh, hell, go ask him yourself."

"He's here?"

"He came in during the floor show. That's him at the corner table. The George Washington of Micronesia."

There were four men sitting at the corner table, all Palauans. Dressed like construction workers, three of them had obviously stopped in for a quick beer on the way home from work and gotten caught. The fourth man was Kintaro.

Booker studied the table for a while, debating whether to approach. After all, Kintaro was spending an evening in his own territory—he was talking to his own people, speaking his native tongue, taking care of his own business. He was also, Booker saw, utterly bored.

The three Palauans gulped down their beers and ordered a fresh beer for Kintaro with every tray. Barely touched, his bottles stacked up in front of him like unkept promises. The others were praising him, interrupting each other to perfect their compliments while Kintaro sat listening, his eyes darting restlessly around the room. The three others would touch him to underscore their admiration—overlong handshakes, arms around his shoulder—but Kintaro did not like to be touched.

"Will he talk to me, if I walk over?" Booker asked the distad.

Dunbar had forgotten Kintaro, had turned back to watch Angie work.

"What's that?" he asked.

"If I walk over and introduce myself to Kintaro, will he talk with me? Is he quotable?"

"Sure, he's quotable. Go ahead."

Booker weaved through the dance floor, beer in hand, and stepped to Kintaro's table.

Kintaro looked up and saw him coming. Their eyes met. Radical he may be, Booker thought, but this is no guerrilla fighter. Though Kintaro ignored the beers in front of him, he was, nonetheless, twenty pounds overweight, and that was plenty of surplus on a short man. The ashtray in front of him was filled with cigarette butts.

The three other Palauans broke off their talk as soon as they realized an outsider was standing at the table.

"Mr. Kintaro?"

"Yes?"

"My name's Marshall Booker, and I'm a reporter for *Gotham* magazine. I came out to do a piece on Red Elwell, and for the past couple days I've been rattling around Peleliu. I'm about ready to head back, but it occurred to me that all the time I'd been here, I hadn't touched base with a real Micronesian. Do you think we could talk?"

"What do we have to talk about?"

If there was power in Kintaro, it was in his face. Not his entire face—already, it was running to fat with the rest of his body—but, more specifically, in his eyes, large and restless, moving from corner to corner, from person to person, like the eyes of an animal trapped in a snare, hopelessly caught, waiting to discover just which hunter had placed the device, had baited it.

"Well, you delivered a mighty interesting speech this afternoon. You mentioned Elwell. What I need is a Micronesian view of the story, of Elwell and what he means to you."

"Just a moment, then," Kintaro said. He turned to the other men and spoke in Palauan, gesturing at Booker. The other three looked up and nodded gravely. The long-nose whom Angie had put on the floor had acquired an identity.

Without another word, Kintaro stood up, grabbed a bottle of Kirin, and led Booker out of the Darling Bar. Turning left, he circled around to the back of the building. There, at the edge of the lagoon, the wreck of an old Japanese dock pointed out into the water.

"If we walk all the way out to the end, we can avoid the mosquitoes," Kintaro said. "There's a good breeze."

Kintaro found a piece of cardboard, placed it on the concrete, and sat down on top of it, careful not to soil his trousers. He handed the beer to Booker.

"Take it. I don't want it. I don't drink beer. But they buy them for me, they insist. The scotch is too expensive."

"Thanks," Booker said. "It's lovely out here. In fact, I've loved my whole stay in Palau. You've got some beautiful islands here."

Kintaro stared straight at Booker, as if he could not believe his ears.

"Did I say something wrong?"

"What do you love about them, Mr. Booker?"

"Well, the scenery, what I've seen of it. That bunch of Rock Islands you pass through on the way to Peleliu, pretty little places, all unspoiled."

"Would you say that Peleliu is a lovely island? Unspoiled? Or Angaur?"

"Well, not exactly. But even so, there's a lot of history there. I wish I could have spent more time out here, and traveled through all the districts."

"Yes, that's regrettable. Mr. Booker, what do you want from me?"

"All right. They say you're a fire-eater. You practically danced a war dance on Elwell's body this afternoon. Sounds like you mean to raise hell in these islands. Is it true?"

"No."

"What?"

"I said no."

"That's all? Just 'no'?"

"That's all."

"You had more to say at the graduation ceremonies. I took notes."

"Okay, Mr. Booker. Elwell was a nothing. If Americans mourn for him, that's their right. And if I want to see something else in his death, I'm entitled. No harm done. It was only a speech."

"What do you see in Elwell's death? That's all I'm asking. What does it mean to you?"

"You've done a little homework, I'm sure. You know the history of these islands. No one has ever asked what we thought, what we wanted. We were pawns—friendly, docile, passive islanders. Wage war on our islands if you like. Protect us or develop us if you like. Try to do both if you like. What could we do about it? One hundred thousand Micronesians living on two thousand islands? Six different cultures, nine totally different languages, and an economy . . ."

"What?"

". . . an economy that last year produced three million dollars in exports. Do you know what they were?"

"Nope."

"Scrap metal. Copra. Handicrafts. Scavenging, coconut picking, and basket weaving. Meanwhile, however, we managed to gobble twenty-five million dollars of imported goods, clothing, cars—you name it. Every year the figures get worse."

"Where does that leave you?"

Kintaro laughed. His eyes gave up on Booker's face and flitted out across the water.

"You said you visited Peleliu. It's not much of a place, is it? Could you live there for the rest of your life? I couldn't. But it's a wealthy island, as islands go out here. There was enough money to send promising students to high school and college. So we went and so we returned. Back we came, along with all the other imports—the canned tuna, the dried fish, the scholarship winners. Am I boring you?"

"No, not a bit," Booker said. But he was not taking notes.

"I think you are bored, Mr. Booker. I think this is all wasted on you. A discussion of Pacific sex life would enliven you. Some stories of betel nut and native dances, a few lines on tattoos and wood carvings."

"No, please."

"I'll finish quickly, and then you can tell your editors you spoke to a real Micronesian. Some of us who came back from Hawaii noticed the irony of our situation. Palau didn't suit us anymore. It was too slow, too traditional, too small. Too hot! We didn't fit. I noticed you watching me in the Darling Bar. I think you saw what I mean. Well, if we could not contend with Palau, we learned something of contending with Americans. We could ask questions about their programs, their purpose. We could throw back at them all the ideals they taught us and which —in an unwise moment—they packaged into the Trusteeship Agreement. Self-determination. Independence. Consent of the governed. We could make them squirm."

"Everybody's squirming down here," Booker said.

"It kills the boredom," Kintaro said. "It makes an interesting game."

"So where does it end? Do you Micronesians want in . . . want to be in the U.S? Or out?"

Kintaro shrugged.

"It's like when your reporters ask your blacks—once and for all now, will it be integration or segregation? In or out? Do they answer you?"

"Okay, so what about Elwell?"

"Nothing," Kintaro said with a yawn. "A footnote. A metaphor. An accidental symbol. Maybe his death marked the end of the old era—the marines crawling over a reef and planting a flag. Maybe he was the last one. Maybe not."

The little quote detector in the back of Booker's head flashed on. At last.

"I could use that," Booker said. "Could I use that?"

"That's all you wanted?" Kintaro laughed. "Well, if you like it, it's yours."

They walked back toward the Darling Bar, but Kintaro did not enter. Instead, he faced Booker and offered his hand.

"I'm not returning to the bar. Payday Friday is new to you. But it gets old fast. Angie will take good care of you, Mr. Booker. Be sure not to miss your plane. Good night."

The toilets were a short walk from the bar, at the edge of the lagoon. They were a matched pair of outhouses, identical roofs, identical floors with identical holes, nearly identical views of the beautiful lagoon above which they perched side by side. Standing over the hole above the beach, Booker wondered why he had encased himself in a frame of wood and metal if his waste was to stream so directly onto the beach below.

Someone fumbled at the door behind him, cursed, and fumbled again.

"It's locked, dammit!" Booker shouted.

"Well, hurry the hell up," a voice said. "Dammit!"

"Just another minute," Booker said with Christlike forbearance.

"Hey, that you, Booker?"

"Yeah. Who's that?"

"Merle Atkinson, baby. Hey, c'mon. What're you, writin' something in there? Let's go!"

Booker opened the door and stepped aside for Atkinson, who rushed inside, dropped his trousers and squatted over the hole. He did not close the door, and he did not mind talking while he sat.

"Where you goin' buddy? Jussa sec. Let me finish. I wanna talk to you."

Booker looked away, concentrating on the moonlight gilding the lagoon which Atkinson so prodigally and noisily befouled.

As they walked back to the Darling Bar, Atkinson dropped his arm around Booker's shoulder and leaned on him. He was dressed in his Friday-night best—the same as his Monday-morning worst—khaki work clothes and engineer's boots caked with mud.

Atkinson was drunk. He smelled of spilled drinks and cigarettes. His movements, so adroit and cunning inside the caves, were disjointed and spastic. Inside the bar, he forced Booker toward a table where a woman was sitting.

"How you like my fucking machine?"

"Jesus, Atkinson, does she understand English? She might not be used to that language."

"Well, now, let's see," Atkinson said.

He leaned over as if to whisper to his woman—a friendly, ugly, monkey-faced woman.

"Fuck, fuck, fuck, fuck, fuck," he whispered gently.

He turned back toward Booker with a good-natured leer.

"I guess she's used to that language now," he grinned. "How do you like her?"

"I think she's a honey." Booker shuddered.

"Been waitin' for weeks to see her," Atkinson confessed. "That whole time we were huntin' Japs, she was in my mind. Know what? We'd be layin' inside some dark tunnel, belly down in bat shit, and I'd think of her. She'd pop into my mind, just automatically. There she'd be."

Touched by his own words, Atkinson reached out a

hand to Monkey-Face. She took his hand in both of hers and lifted it to her face, raw knuckles and caked fingers brushing her lips.

"She knows just what I want," Atkinson said.

Booker tried to smile at the two of them. Monkey-Face was quietly biting the knuckles on Atkinson's hand, and the demolitions chief was getting more and more excited.

"I'm sure you suit each other just fine," Booker forced himself to say.

That was a mistake. There had been a dash too much irony in Booker's voice, and Atkinson had caught it. He yanked his fist out of Monkey-Face's mouth and grasped Marshall Booker by his blue silk shirt, pulling him halfway across the table.

"Don't you talk down to me, you dumb sonofabitch. I could help you if I wanted to."

"Sorry, Merle."

"You shit on my woman, you shit on me, understand? Guilt by association!"

"Understood. No need to hassle after what we've been through. Buy you and your lady a drink?"

The waitress who came to the table was Angie. By now, Booker had decided that he could not pass her up: not because of her looks, but because of her abundance, the challenge of satisfying her, a middleweight's dream of staying ten rounds with a heavyweight. He slid his arm around her waist. She did not move away. Booker moved his hand caressingly and felt the night's heat coming out of her body, her sweat meeting his palm as it moved over her dress. A big woman. No nuances and gentility here, no foreplay and seduction. Pure trucking.

Another waitress returned with the tray of drinks, sliding the paper cups around the table. When Booker looked over his shoulder to call Angie, she was lost in conversation with the distad. She did not hear him.

"Here's to you, Merle, and to your lady," Booker said as the three paper cups bumped and splashed above the oilcloth. "What was it you said about helping me? 'Course, you have been helping me all along. Is that what you meant?"

The two lovers were kissing and fondling each other. Their mouths met, their tongues played hockey with a maraschino cherry, pushing it back and forth. Monkey-Face scored the goal, and Atkinson swallowed the puck.

" 'Scuse us! What was it?"

"You said—I think you said—you could help me."

"Bet your ass I could," Atkinson said, immediately resuming his adoration of Monkey-Face. The two of them stumbled to the dance floor, where they leaned and groped, while Booker waited impatiently. It annoyed him to sit with these swooning drunks. And besides, it was time for him to play let's-make-a-deal with Angie.

It was last call at the Darling Bar, and waitresses picked their way between tables, carrying drinks, awakening drunks. Outside the door, a couple of local police watched out for fights. On the dance floor, a Palauan man in a Nehru jacket sang "I Left My Heart in San Francisco."

"Come on, Merle," he said when the dancers returned. "If you can help me, help me. If you can't, or if you don't want to, let me off the hook. Just don't keep me sitting here. I've got arrangments to make, too."

"Okay," Atkinson said. "I don't like you. I didn't like you when I was sober, and you don't look any better to me when I'm drunk. I think you're a snotty, smooth-talkin' jackoff artist, hear? But that was a bullshit deal goin' down on Peleliu. I was hopin' you'd figger it out for yourself, the way reporters are supposed to put things together. But I got an idea you ain't such a hot reporter after all."

"All right, Merle. Lay it on me."

"The fat guy in the caves—the Palauan—I don't know about. Maybe he had somethin' to do with Elwell. Maybe he just got caught in the caves and panicked. But when I drove out to the runway that night, I saw three, four men around that poor bastard. 'Member that?"

"Sure. They ran off into the mountains, you said."

"Right. And by the end of the next day, we had Colonel Vincent with us, and we were fightin' World War II again. And what could I do with Vincent, that nut? He'd look for lips on a chicken! Stragglers! I knew we wouldn't find no stragglers! But I went along with the program, takin' care of my little concession on the side. And if you write one damn word about that end of it, I'll come find you wherever the hell you are and make you sorry! I'll come to New York City! Understand?"

"Okay, Merle, I'll leave your business alone."

"Well, like I say, I played along with Vincent. I said to myself, I said, stay cool, Merle, don't say nothin', don't say shit if your mouth's full of it. So I just set back and let it all happen, till we were all standin' there and Vincent was scratchin' his head tryin' to figger out who he'd killed. That's when I got wise."

"Wise to what?"

"I saw what a crock the whole operation was. I got home that night, and I found somethin' that started me thinkin' it all through. And I figgered who did it, and now I'm gonna tell you. I'm gonna tell you first who *didn't* do it."

"Well, not the Japanese. That much we know."

"The hell they didn't! Little polite yellow people,

bowing and scraping and walking around in groups with their knapsacks and cameras! They did it! Here!"

Atkinson handed Booker an envelope. Inside was a Polaroid photograph. It showed a group of men, Palauan laborers mostly, posing in front of Atkinson's house on Peleliu, grinning and drinking beer. Among them, a head taller than the rest, smiling uncomfortably, stood Red Elwell.

"The bone hunters did it," Atkinson said. "Not the stragglers."

"The *what?*"

"Ah hah! They didn't even tell you 'bout them! I bet they didn't! For two weeks before Elwell came, there was a bunch of Japanese hunting around Peleliu, gatherin' bones of their beloved. They'd follow us around from day to day, the morbid bastards. They took that picture the afternoon before they killed Elwell."

"Whoa, hold it. The picture doesn't prove that!"

"They recognized him, man! They wanted him in the picture! Bet you there's a big print of this shot in some Nip trophy room now. Know somethin' else, somethin' that really churns my guts? Our own guys know about it!"

"The Americans!"

"Hell, yes! Next morning, just before Vincent flew in, some marines came down and evacuated the Japanese double quick. They called off the rest of the bone hunt and flew 'em all the hell out of there."

"Why do that?"

"You are one slow thinker, aren't you? To cover their trail, that's why. The chickenshit government doesn't have the guts to stick it to the Japs. They know who did it, but they don't want to risk a flap. Some desk jockey on Guam probably slaps his forehead and says, wow, shouldn't have let Elwell visit while the bone hunters were there, but accidents will happen. So the whitewash begins. The real murderers get off, and we go chasin' ghosts!"

"Can I keep this picture?"

"Hell, yes, I've got no use for it. I'm a little guy. A junkman. But it pisses me off. They come visitin', on their best behavior. They don't drink, don't screw, keep off the grass. Till they spot that dumb drunk Elwell visitin' my house. Then, powee, it's Pearl Harbor all over again! Kill time!"

Booker tucked the picture back into the envelope and placed it in his shirt pocket. He dearly hoped that it was all true. It embellished his story in a way that tantalized him. It stacked irony on irony in a pattern that he would enjoy describing. If it were true, close to true, not palpably false, it would be the story that shook things up, that came trailing prizes and book contracts. Elwell's murder by stragglers was compelling enough. His killing by contemporary Japanese, the avenging relatives of Elwell's long-dead victims, was sensational. And, coupled with an embarrassed government's cover-up, it was dynamite.

The Darling Bar was almost empty, yet Angie was nowhere to be seen. Another barmaid shrugged when he mentioned her name and told him to leave.

"Go and come back tomorrow," she said. The tired barmaid's ever-green promise.

Booker had blown it, he thought, by leaving to interview Kintaro, by sitting with Atkinson and Monkey-Face, by losing himself in conversation.

He watched the cars empty out of the lot, beer bottles smashing against rocks at the edge of the lagoon, the jukebox dying in midsong in the darkened bar behind him.

Inez, it will be, he thought, stumbling along the road back to the hotel. And then, a little reporting trip to Japan.

The car pulled out from behind the bar, climbed onto the road, and had almost passed when it came to a sudden halt, then backed toward him.

"Hop in," Dunbar called to him. "I'll drop you at the hotel."

Booker ran around to the opposite side of the car and opened the front door.

There sat Angie.

"The back door," the distad said. "Sit in back."

As soon as he got in, Booker leaned forward, placing his head between the barmaid and the distad.

"I'll be damned," he said. "Hello there, Angie."

Angie said something in Palauan. Her voice had gone flat.

"I think she's saying that it's very late, time for everybody to go home, come back again tomorrow night, words to that effect," Dunbar said.

"Yeah, I know," Booker said. "But I'll bet you don't have to come back tomorrow night. I'll bet you're having your party tonight. While your wife's on Guam."

"Lay off, Booker. I'm just taking the lady home. To her kids."

"Well, I'll just come along for the ride," Booker said. "Maybe Angie will want me to be dropped off with her. Meet the kids and all."

"You're getting off here," said the distad, pulling into the driveway of the hotel. "I'm not driving four miles out of my way to prove anything to you."

"Sure, sure, sure," Booker said. "Sweet dreams."

"The airport bus leaves from in front of the hotel at 6:30. That's about four hours."

A short burst of Palauan from Angie. What was it with her? Too tired to speak English? English during business hours only?

"Angie wishes you a good flight," the distad said.

SIX
THE BONE HUNTERS

I

Like a deep-sea diver rising off the ocean floor, Booker awoke slowly, in stages, groping into lighter water, blinking at the dazzling surface of a new day.

Inez was gone. That, for the time being, was no loss. Their reunion on Guam had sated him. She had been worth waiting for, and it now seemed inconceivable that he could have panted after the slatternly Angie when an air-conditioned room, a wide bed, and a willing Inez had waited for him here.

Booker lifted himself out of bed with a groan. If he ate nothing but oysters, eggs, black bread, and steak tartar, if he chewed garlic by the clove, he might—just might—reestablish communication with his exhausted libido in a month or so.

Nothing he had asked for had surprised Inez, nothing had tired her, nothing had required explanation. Her climaxes had splashed down like a rich man's coins into a church collection plate.

Booker stepped to the balcony, pulled back the curtain, opened the door, and walked out into un-air-conditioned Guam.

She was easy to find. Leaning against a palm, Inez

had established herself as the star of the Dai Ichi Hotel swimming pool. A phalanx of Japanese men surrounded her, snapping away at the island girl with their cameras, probing with light meters, unbundling tripods. Abandoned, an equal number of Japanese women sat around the pool, short and flat-chested, their fish-white skin scorched and blistered like pizza. No wonder their men grabbed their cameras and rushed toward Inez. Pictures of their own women might interest a dermatologist, might decorate a hospital burn ward, might draw crowds at a med-school slide show, but that was it.

Booker slipped on his trunks and took the elevator downstairs. Among the poolside burn victims, tubes of salve, and too-late sunbonnets, there were angry mutterings. The Japanese men had coaxed Inez into posing with her arm around this or that member of the group. This, she had willingly done. She looked as if she had just spent an exquisite night with each of the smiling, spindly legged little tourists who popped up against her cleavage.

Booker coolly stepped right into the pictures, leading Inez off to the side of the pool.

"You not mind?" Inez asked solicitously. "They say they wanted pictures to take home."

"Sure they do," Booker answered darkly, thinking of Elwell's picture, rolled up inside some Japanese Nikon. "They've got to have that picture."

"What did you say?"

"The Japanese people have a thing about taking pictures. They take pictures of everything."

"They said they liked me for their pictures," Inez said. "I think they said they liked my body."

"No kidding?"

Inez laughed, leaned over Booker, and began rubbing his body with oil. They were on a grassy knoll midway between the pool and the ocean. Behind them was a sort of outdoor pavilion, covered with thatch and made to look like a Tahitian meetinghouse. From inside the Tahitian hut came the sound of electric guitars.

"How did you know to meet me at the airport?" Booker asked.

"Your friend say I should."

"Beckman?"

"Yes, your friend."

"What else did Beckman tell you?"

Inez giggled a little and slapped Booker with her hands, as if he should know better than to tease her this way.

"No, tell me," he insisted. "What did Beckman say?"

"Like last time," Inez said. She was bothered by this talk. She kept her eyes down, concentrating on kneading the small of his back. She worked hard at it, turning the application of suntan oil into a professional massage. A bead of sweat trickled down between her breasts.

"What do you mean, like last time?"

"That I should go with you. And do what you wanted."

"And he would pay you?"

She nodded.

"How much, Inez? What was the price for what we did in the car?"

She didn't answer. Maybe it was none of his business.

"And for this time—how many nights will he pay for?" Booker asked. "If I stay for a week, it's all for free?"

Again, no reply.

"Listen, then," Booker said, turning onto his back so he could face her. "Last time, we forget about. But from now on, whatever it costs—whatever *you* cost—

I pay. You tell me, and I'll pay. Keep track of it. And you charge me just what you charge him. No less."

She thought it over for a while, reflectively rubbing his chest, slicking down the hair. She liked the hair on his chest.

"Why?" she asked. "Is simple, the old way. We have fun and your friend pay."

Booker rose, stopped her hands in midstroke, and made sure he was looking in her eyes.

"No, Inez," he explained. "It is not a good system. One favor between friends is okay. But if Beckman pays for everything, then I will owe him something. A big favor. I don't want to owe him a big favor. Understand?"

"Okay," she said. "I work for you. But . . ."

"What?"

"I am expensive."

"How much?"

A pause followed, and when the answer came, it had two voices.

"Very expensive," Inez said, first.

"Damned expensive," Major Beckman echoed. "If you have to ask what this yacht costs, you can't afford it."

Beckman stood above them, the smiling proprietor of their romance. He wore civilian clothes today, had a *Harper's* magazine tucked under his arm and a Cigarillo in his mouth. He was the image of a best man who had dropped by to make sure that his honeymooners' nuptial night had gone passably well.

Beckman still had clout with Inez. He gestured toward the beach, and, without a word, Inez dropped the suntan oil, slipped off her sandals, and bounded toward the surf.

"You say scram, she scrams, that it?" Booker asked resentfully.

"What's the matter, buddy?" Beckman asked. "Sounds like you got a bug up your ass."

"From here on, I'll pay."

"Fair enough," Beckman replied accommodatingly. "You want to pay for her, you go ahead. You get her to give it to you for nothing, I'll buy you a drink. You marry her, I'll dance at your wedding. Okay?"

Booker kept his silence, staring out at the brown girl in the pink bathing suit.

"But that's not all that's bothering you, is it?" Beckman asked. "You didn't answer my message to call. I told Inez to tell you. I left a message at the hotel desk last night, and this morning. But no call."

"I had my good reasons for not calling you," Booker answered. "I still do. I'm onto that fast shuffle you guys pulled on Peleliu. From here on out, the less we have to say to each other, the better."

"Fast shuffle on Peleliu?" Beckman asked incredulously. "Did I hear you right?"

"You sure did."

"Colonel Vincent involved in a fast shuffle? A slow shuffle, maybe . . ."

"Maybe you were in on it. Maybe not. But somebody was pulling tricks down there. And it wasn't Colonel Vincent."

"A trick," Beckman said, almost to himself. "And a shuffle."

He sat down beside Booker and buried his Cigarillo in the sand.

"Would you believe," Beckman finally resumed, "would you believe that I haven't the faintest idea what you're talking about?"

"I might," Booker answered indifferently. "It's a big ocean."

"No, it's a small island. Something went on, I should know about it."

"That's too bad," Booker said.

The Japanese photographers had sighted Inez again and crept behind the palms bordering the beach. They pointed their Nikons out at her from behind tree trunks, aiming like snipers.

"Hey, Booker!"

It was Beckman again, interrupting his reveries.

"I'm asking you what happened down there. Just a thumbnail sketch. Can you give me that much?"

"What's in it for me, Major? This story could be a mover and a shaker. I can't go giving it away. Look, buddy, we get along. You know that. But we're in different rackets. We sit on opposite sides of the table."

"You want a deal?"

"If you can make one. I don't think you can."

"Okay, try this. You tell me what happened. I'll try to tell you who set it up—who planned it, approved it, did it. It'll take some work, but I'll give you the part of the story you don't have."

Booker snapped to attention. The story he had pictured divided into three parts; and so far, he was sure of only two. The first third was about Elwell and Peleliu, the battleground stuff, the caves, the local color. The second part he could get in Japan—the identity, the mentality, and the background of the bone hunters. If he couldn't get it, he could fake it.

The third segment—the hardest—was still missing: the cover-up, the role of the Americans who had whisked the Japanese visitors away, trading the real culprits for Colonel Vincent and his straggler fantasies.

"You'll give me the names?" Booker asked. "American names?"

"American names."

"On paper?"

"I'll find the documents. I'll put my ass on the line for you."

"Not just clerk-typists. I want officers."

"You'll have it, as far up as it goes on Guam. Do we have a deal?"

Booker looked over at Beckman and felt a renewal of their old camaraderie, like the night he had met Inez. Whom else did Booker know who would talk like this, trade like this, with no bullshit appeals to patriotism, no invocations of friendship, only the straight quid pro quo?

"Yes. We have a deal. Now, Major, brace yourself to take some notes, and I'll tell you what happened in your own backyard."

II

After Beckman left the hotel, the weather turned muggy and oppressive. The journalist and his woman retired to their air-conditioned room for lunch and a matinée. Replenishing and depleting him, Inez was Sisyphean in her approach to sex. Painstakingly, she would work up the heavy weight of his libido, rolling the boulder back to old heights, delighted in an inch's progress, only to have the whole thing come tumbling back down in one quick rush, and the whole labor to begin again. There was no end to her willingness.

Relaxing, watching Inez at the bottom of their mountain, Booker reflected that he was again in control of the story and of his life. Beckman was doubtless sweating out phone calls, crashing open file cabinets, rummaging through in-boxes, reporting the hardest part of the story for him. They were both working for Marshall Booker—Beckman and Inez. He was reminded of that luminous Beverly Hills morning not long ago, when he had dictated a story while a woman rooted between his legs. It mattered to him, this tie-up between his women and his writing. Although he had never figured out the connection, he knew he had to have them both. Inez was a valid expense-account item, whatever she cost. Abstinence, sacrifice, isolation were not a condition of his trade. The men who locked themselves into rooms to write, who trained like athletes for their stories, kidded themselves about journalism—which was not a consecrated art. And they came out of their labors looking foolish, these solemn artists, fatuous as if they had rented tuxedoes for a visit to a highway diner.

A rap on the door had found Inez halfway up the slope.

"Who is it?" Booker shouted.

"It's me," Beckman answered. "With my end of the deal."

"So soon?"

"Not quite. We're going to have to take a twenty-minute plane trip. I'll fill you in along the way. Say, can I come in?"

"Not yet," Booker shouted. Inez had redoubled her efforts, determined to work her way up to the peak. "Wait down the hall."

Now, two islands floated below the plane. The farther island—Saipan—was long and rugged, its green-brown slopes piling up into a cone-shaped mountain, as if some homesick Japanese had constructed a minature Mount Fuji.

The nearer island was Tinian. As the plane flew over

the northern end, losing altitude, Booker glimpsed four runways, far longer and wider than the Peleliu strips. They passed over these—over an ugly, burned-looking savannah of brush and pine—and finally set down on one of the two smaller runways at the middle of the island. These strips were cluttered with construction trailers, survey equipment, stacked oil drums, tool sheds, bulldozers.

Their pilot disappeared in one jeep. Beckman motioned to another.

"I hope this trip has a point," Booker warned. Hot winds blew down the runway like blasts from an open oven. "It's hotter than hell."

"There's a point, all right," Beckman answered. "Take this for openers."

He reached into his pocket for a sealed envelope and handed it to Booker.

"You said you wanted the name of the man who evacuated those Jap bone hunters off Peleliu. The man in charge of the cover-up. The American name, I think you said."

Booker tore open the envelope, read the contents, looked up in a surprise that was mingled with fear.

"You did it?"

"That's my card. I'm the guilty party. I confess. You'd better stop me before I kill again."

"Why couldn't you tell me this on Guam? What'd you bring me to this godforsaken island for?"

"You curious . . . or nervous?"

"What are we doing here?"

"Just hush up, will you?"

Beckman started the jeep before Booker could respond, and they went careening down the runway, dodging fallen trees, avoiding clumps of undergrowth.

"What's going on here!?" Booker shouted.

Beckman snapped on a radio, roaming up and down the whole band until he bracketed the only station, an Armed Forces Network show being rebroadcast from Saipan. Nancy Sinatra whelped about boots made for walking over people.

They sped down along a highway toward the end of the island. On one side, cattle grazed among old Japanese pillboxes.

"You're on Broadway," Beckman said out of nowhere. He sounded cheerful.

Booker did not answer. He was tired of framing questions that might or might not get replies. He was not in control of the game now. The morning's feeling of supremacy, of Beckman and Inez both at his mercy, had evaporated.

"Tinian has this funny resemblance to Manhattan," Beckman continued. "When they laid out the roads in 1944, they duplicated the map of New York City—Eighth Avenue, Fifth Avenue, Forty-second and One hundred and tenth. Hundreds of miles of road. All gone now, except for Broadway."

Broadway was in trouble. Two of the four lanes disappeared behind ranks of saplings, fought to reemerge, then vanished for good. The remaining lanes curved and dipped as the tangan-tangan strained to complete an overhead arch. Beckman turned left onto a dirt track through even denser vegetation. Another turn—a right, this time—brought them onto a recently bulldozed track through a low, dry meadow. Now they were listening to the "Grand Ole Opry," from Nashville.

The dirt track led them out onto the first major runway, a hot, solid river of stone—unmarked, empty, silent except for gusts of hot wind.

Beckman seemed lost. He drove slowly, looking over the edge of his jeep, as if he were searching for footprints. Then he found what he wanted—bright yellow arrows clumsily daubed on the runway—and he picked up speed again, following the arrows. They drove across all four runways, then down a windy road which ended in two open spaces, each the size of a parking lot.

Set right in the middle of each lot, about two hundred yards apart, were twin monuments, or markers, or tombstones: metal plates fastened onto white cement pedestals. To the rear of each was a kind of garden, a rectangular plot with ivy, a palm tree, and a yellow-blossomed plumeria.

Near one of the monuments, a dozen people had assembled, surrounding a stack of bleached firewood.

"Where are we?" Booker asked.

"The A-bomb pits. The *Enola Gay* and her sister were loaded here. Where that garden is now, they hoisted the bombs up into the belly of the plane. You can read about it yourself."

The plate glinted in the sun:

FROM THIS LOADING PIT THE FIRST ATOMIC BOMB EVER TO BE USED IN COMBAT WAS LOADED ABOARD A B-29 AIRCRAFT AND DROPPED ON HIROSHIMA, JAPAN, AUGUST 6, 1945. THE BOMBER, PILOTED BY COLONEL PAUL W. TIBBETS, JR., USAAF, OF THE 509TH COMPOSITE GROUP, TWENTIETH AIR FORCE, UNITED STATES ARMY AIR FORCES, WAS LOADED LATE IN THE AFTERNOON OF AUGUST 4, 1945, AND AT 0245 THE FOLLOWING MORNING TOOK OFF ON ITS MISSION. CAPTAIN WILLIAM S. PARSONS, USN, WAS ABOARD AS WEAPONEER.

"It's not John Hersey, but it shows some restraint," Beckman commented.

"What's the other marker say?"

"Same thing, only for Nagasaki. Want to walk over?"

"No. Who are the tourists around the firewood?"

"You're wrong on two counts, Scoop. Those are not tourists, and that is not firewood."

Booker squinted through the shimmering heat waves that danced above the runway and focused on the gathering. He recoiled in surprise.

The bones were stacked like firewood, log-cabin style, with the heavier limbs at the bottom of the structure, the lighter bones in the middle, and skulls at the very top. A thin plume of black smoke was curling off the pile.

The group stepped back as soon as the fire began. The heat that soaked into the runway from the sun was itself enough to turn gum shoes sticky. With the fire added, the heat must have been unbearable. As they moved back, slowly, haltingly, almost as if they were reluctant to separate themselves from the pile of bones, Booker saw that the people were Japanese. He could hear snatches of the song they were singing.

"Bone hunters?"

"Right. Japanese bone hunters. And—to answer your next question—it's the very same team who were on Peleliu the night Elwell was killed. They were evacuated the next morning on my orders."

Booker stared at the Japanese. The fire was collapsing in on itself, skulls falling through ribs and limbs, rolling onto the floor of the runway.

He had not expected the Japanese to be so old and frail. So small, so stoop-shouldered, so white-haired. Nor had he expected to find them like this, lifting frail voices in a quavering funeral anthem. They were Japanese, but they had nothing in common with stragglers, nothing in common with the people he had hoped to find, nothing in common with the affluent, giggling tourists baking and molting on the patio of the Dai Ichi Hotel. These Japanese were permanently traumatized, hopelessly out of touch with postwar Japan. They were as pathetic, as burned-out as Elwell himself had been. They were old.

"Come meet your murder suspects," Beckman invited him. "Let's go bust 'em."

"Hey, forget that," Booker said. "It was a bum steer."

"But how can we be sure? Let's check it out. Hey, Father Richards!"

Beckman had called out to a tall, husky American who was standing among the Japanese mourners. The man looked up and waved back, signaling that he would join them in a moment. He carefully poured a cup of gasoline out of a red five-gallon can, stepped forward, and threw the contents onto the smoldering pyre, setting off a fresh conflagration. Then he came puffing toward the two Americans.

"Major Beckman! A pleasure!"

"How's your work, Padre?"

"Almost finished here, as you can see, thank God. It's almighty hot."

"Did they find much?"

"More than they had expected to. There were good caves. I think that they appreciate being permitted to come to Tinian. Earlier, they'd been given to believe that it would be off-limits. I suppose we have you to thank for the change in the policy."

"It took some doing," Beckman conceded.

"Well, our friends are grateful. But they would like to return to Peleliu on another trip someday."

"I'm sure it can be arranged. Father, this is Mr. Marshall Booker, a journalist. He's been visiting us, researching a piece on Red Elwell."

Booker shook hands with the Jesuit. If his face was red, his nose was scarlet, bulbous, pitted, and streaked by tiny veins which wiggled like amoeba on a laboratory slide.

"Booker here came across some Palau gossip . . ."

"You've got to watch that Palau talk." Father Richards laughed. "Everybody talks down there. Everybody! Including me! What'd they say?"

"He got a bug in his ear about Elwell's killing. He reasons that since we didn't find any stragglers, maybe some other Japanese did it. Like some of those bone collectors you've been escorting."

It was as if the Jesuit had been shot. "The bone collectors did it! Of course! That's marvelous! And how did they do it, pray tell? Stab him to death with a walking cane? Garrot him with an elastic bandage?"

Booker stood there, sweating and feeling small. It was like having an editor kill a story.

"Well, lad," the Jesuit continued, "look at our Japanese visitors. They're no stragglers. They're too old for that! These are the parents and widows of grown men who were killed twenty-five years ago. Do you understand? Their average age is sixty-one, their average physical condition is poor, and their average mood is morbid. They're a walking geriatric ward."

"Just for the record, Padre," Beckman said, "what did the Japanese do when they finished work in the boondocks?"

"Work? They didn't work. That Mr. Atkinson had the bones ready for them. They made an arrangement with him. He did the work."

"He did it for nothing?" Booker asked.

"That I wouldn't know," the Jesuit answered. "But

whatever they arranged, I'm sure everybody was happy. Those people are in no condition to climb into caves!"

"Same question as before, Padre," Beckman persisted. "What did they do the night Elwell was killed?"

"That was our last night on Peleliu, wasn't it?" the Jesuit said. "Not that anybody knew it at the time. Well, it was just like any other night. They returned around seven from Atkinson's house, where they had gone to find out about procedure for the next day. They bathed, relaxed, had a light supper, and went to bed. And there they stayed."

"Can you be sure? How do you know?" Beckman enjoyed the inquisitorial role.

"Because I stayed up reading, as I do every night. Reading, and walking a bit around the camp. It was a lovely moonlit night, I recall."

"Did you hear Atkinson's jeep go by?"

"I certainly did. I remember thinking that the demolitions chief was up to his usual concupiscence."

"After the jeep passed, what then?"

"More silence, more reading, more little walks. Everybody was sleeping, believe me. The tents were open. I could see their faces in the moonlight. And the jeep remained parked in front of my tent."

"Are you sure of all this, Padre?"

"Absolutely."

Beckman looked at Booker.

"Had enough?"

"Enough," Booker said, offering the Jesuit his hand. "I was misled."

"You've got to watch the way people talk on islands," Father Richards said.

They were sitting at the four-stool bar of the rickety wooden structure called the Tinian Hotel. Several typhoons ago, Beckman said, the empty U-shaped building had been General Curtis Le May's headquarters. He pointed to a nearby table where the general's choleric, cigar-smoking face poked out from the cover of *Time*. He had been given favored position among the out-of-date magazines.

The hotel proprietor, an elderly Marshallese, served them their beer and disappeared.

"Let's get down to business," Beckman said. "I told you I moved those Japanese off Peleliu as soon as I heard Elwell was murdered. But I didn't tell you why."

"I know it wasn't to cover up," Booker hastened to say.

"Thanks for the vote of confidence," Beckman said. "But I'll bet you still can't guess—can't begin to imagine—why I did it."

"No," Booker admitted.

"Journalists. I can't figure you guys out. Always straining for a complicated explanation when there's a simple answer staring you in the face. Looking for a plot, a cover-up, a conspiracy. What is it with you guys? Even you! Especially you!"

"I made a mistake, and I . . ."

"I moved those Japs out of there as an act of plain charity. Humanity. Mercy. Words like that. With no strings attached. I knew that the bone hunters were on Peleliu, and as soon as I heard about the killing, I knew Colonel Vincent would make the scene. He's been waiting for years to go on a straggler hunt, and he isn't getting any younger. Are you with me so far? Would you like another beer?"

"No."

"*I* would," Beckman said. He slid around to the back of the bar and served himself. He stayed behind the partition, leaning forward on his elbows like a bartender.

"Okay, there I sat on Guam, thinking, oh, shit, what

if Vincent is right—what if stragglers did knock Elwell off? What would it be like for those old bone hunters to see the war break out again in front of their eyes, to watch Colonel Vincent rip those stragglers up? Imagine it! They come looking for dry bones and are suddenly confronted with the possibility that some of their flesh and blood may still be alive. And, what's more, they may see those very kinsmen hunted down and killed, flushed out and shot like rabbits! Can you imagine a worse torture?"

"No," Booker agreed. "Discover that your long-lost son is still alive and then see him die."

"So you understand," Beckman said, clapping his friend on the shoulder. "I intervened. I had them moved off Peleliu. When you came, I got you fed, drunk, and—I hate to remind you—*very* well laid. And I set you up with an exclusive on the whole Peleliu hunt. So what happens? You crap on me!"

Beckman glanced at Booker. He had expected his monologue to be interrupted by now, but the journalist was taking it all in.

"Goes to show you what happens when you play it straight," Beckman resumed. "Believe me, these islands are a busy enough bailiwick as it is. You saw the work we're doing on the runways here, and that's just the beginning. I didn't ask for a planeload of Japanese old-timers. I didn't ask for Red Elwell to be poured through here. I didn't ask for you to come in and make like some red-hot newshawk from the *Washington Post*."

He poured himself another beer, the melancholy barkeep whom all the world troubled for the price of a drink.

"Look," Booker said in a flat, hushed voice. "I was wrong. I owe you."

"What?"

"I owe you an apology."

"Skip it."

"No, this has got to be said. If I'd made the same mistake with someone else, or closer to home, I wouldn't apologize, but you're my friend . . ."

"And we're alone here at the end of the world, so the word won't get around . . ."

"That, too. Just let me say it. Reporters . . . we blow it sometimes. We always depend on other people, and if most of them had a brain, they wouldn't talk to us in the first place. So we extract our little quotes, snip our evidence, work up a couple of paragraphs of description, and we glue the bullshit together and put our name on it."

"It's your trade, buddy. Profession."

"Sure, but we go wrong."

"Is this *the* Marshall Booker? The circulation builder?"

Booker laughed. "Yeah. But don't quote me. Just remember I said I was sorry."

"Stop apologizing. Contrition is bullshit!"

"It's just that I think there's a certain number of people in the world who've had some contact with reporters, and most of them are pissed off as a result. Pretty soon, the only ones left who'll talk to us are lawyers, fired employees, and flacks."

"I'm not a disgruntled employee, and I'm no flack. I *am* a lawyer, but that's beside the point. I'm you're friend. You want to remember that."

"I'll remember."

"Then let's get back to Where America's Day Begins. You and your woman primed for some steaks tonight? Compliments of the military-industrial complex?"

"Sure. But the Eastern-liberal media elite is buying."

"Wow," said Beckman, laughing. "How things have changed!"

II

They returned to the mini-America of Guam, the American colony that dreamed secret dreams of statehood and supinely spread its legs to cruise ships and tourists, to bombers and bored servicemen.

And Booker returned to Inez, who leaped off the bed to greet him and yet sneaked glances at the TV while Booker pumped and sweated over her. For the first time, Booker wondered how much she was costing.

The phone interrupted him.

"Big change of plans," Beckman whispered.

"No steaks?"

"Steaks, sure. But not on Guam. Get packing. And pack your lady, too. We're going back to Palau."

"You mean *you're* going back to Palau. I'm going back to bed."

"Not when I read you this confidential cable I've got in front of me."

"No cable on earth would get me back to that place. I've worked too hard on this story already."

"If I don't read it to you, I'll have to leak it to someone else. One of the wire-service guys. It's your move."

"Damn it. Okay, read it."

INVESTIGATION HERE INDICATES FRANCISCO KINTARO HEADED MURDER PLOT AGAINST ELWELL STOP KINTARO CONFINED PALAU JAIL STOP SUBSTANTIAL LOCAL UNREST STOP PLEASE ADVISE STOP THOMAS DUNBAR, DISTAD PALAU

PART THREE

SEVEN
ON GEISHA LANE

I

They had barely lifted off the runway at Guam when Inez fell asleep against Marshall Booker's shoulder. Her hand nestled on the upper part of his leg. Was that familiarity or trust? Booker wondered.

The idea of transplanting Inez to New York grew more and more appealing. Booker knew there would be problems—the shift of language and culture, the acceptance of city life, the change of climate. She would not be able to talk about books, and she would not understand films; she would not like his sardonic Manhattan friends. Faced with all these changes, she might sit at home, eat candy, and watch television.

But the advantages were substantial. She was, by a wide margin, the finest woman Booker had ever had. He had never really gotten on with the intense, competitive, harassed women of Manhattan. He did not want an intellectual co-pilot; he would do the thinking for both of them. He did not want to come home at night and discuss his stories. When it came to women, Booker's requirements were simple: that they be beautiful, leave him his freedom, and not say anything stupid in the presence of people who mattered. If that meant keeping their mouths shut, sitting in silence, that was okay, too.

Even if Inez failed, if she got fat or homesick, the cost of liquidating the arrangement would be minimal. He could give her a few thousand, one lawyerless lump sum, and put her on an aloha flight to Honolulu.

II

In just a few days, District Administrator Thomas Dunbar had aged ten years.

When Booker met him at the high school commencement, the tall, tanned distad had seemed to combine exotic living and bourgeois comfort like a successful beachcomber. Now he seemed distracted and unsure of himself. Pale and drawn, he barely glanced at Inez—and that was a sure sign of illness. On the road to Koror, he drove in silence, staying close to the police jeep in front, keeping his Oldsmobile camouflaged in a cloud of dust.

In front of the distad's house sat a squad of Palauan policemen. Booker wondered whether they were there to protect the distad or imprison him.

"Did my wife contact you on Guam?" the distad asked Beckman.

"No," Beckman answered flatly.

"I told her. I radioed her. To see if you could bring her back on your flight."

"I contacted her all right. Out at her sister's house on Tamuning."

"And?"

"She wants to spend a few more days on Guam."

"That means she's heard about Kintaro," the distad said.

"How could that be?" Beckman asked. "There's been

nothing on the radio or in the newspapers."

"Never mind. The coconut telegraph. She's a Palauan. She heard. She's a Palauan first. And then my wife."

"That shouldn't bother *you*, Dunbar," Booker taunted. "A midnight mover like yourself."

Beckman frowned, wincing at Booker's jibe. But it was all lost on the distad. He was gazing out across the lawn, down at the bay and the limestone islands. The same view he had seen every night and morning for twenty years, only now it did not please him.

Beckman cleared his throat and got down to business. "Now what's all this about Kintaro?"

The suspicion began the night of the commencement ceremonies, the distad told them. Perhaps suspicion was too strong. Call it a feeling of being ill at ease, a sense of plotting, an intimation that he and everyone else in Palau were being manipulated.

As a white American bureaucrat assigned to the government of brown aliens on conquered islands, Dunbar had never quite lost the feeling that he was essentially a colonial official. When he had first come to Palau, he had been cautious—overly cautious—in seeing that his dealings with Palauans were as open as he could make them. He had sought their approval where none had ever been asked, even at the cost of delaying or canceling important capital improvements while they debated. He had purged the handful of ex-marine rednecks who called adult Palauans "boy." He had scared off the anthropologists, the wearers of pith helmets. And, although he had not done so to win popular support, he had married a Palauan woman after the collapse of his first marriage.

Dunbar had expected that the most hostility would come from the Palauans who had worked with, and respected, the departed Japanese. He was wrong. These Palauans—middle-level civil servants, policemen, school principals, village magistrates—easily managed the transition to American rule, just as easily as they would have handled a shift from American rule to Chinese. Or Mexican. And the hereditary chiefs, whom he had also worried about, were no problem. The Japanese had intimidated these village patriarchs, had run roughshod over caste systems, land tenure patterns, local power structures. The handful of American custodians, headed by Tom Dunbar, posed no such threat. Before long, everyone had relaxed.

Trouble, when it came, originated in another, wholly unexpected quarter: the young, American-educated Palauans, the scholarship students, the political science majors. Kintaro.

"That's interesting enough," Beckman interrupted him. The distad's narrative was going too slowly. "But that kind of feeling—that militancy—was bound to come. You didn't throw Kintaro in jail for being militant? For delivering a speech? Did you?"

"The speech was only the beginning," Dunbar said. "But don't forget it. How he used Elwell in that speech. How he played on people's being upset with Colonel Vincent's operation down on Peleliu."

"I won't forget," Beckman promised. "But get on with it."

"The morning after the speech, I got a radio message from Peleliu," Dunbar continued. "Colonel Vincent wanted to see me. He was sending a boat to pick me up."

"Did he say what for?"

"Only that it was urgent. That I was not to send anyone else in my place. And that I was to come alone."

Dunbar had met a gloomy Colonel Vincent at the camp on Orange Beach. Together, they had traveled in silence over the straits to the Coast Guard station on Angaur.

They walked past the barracks, through the mess hall, and stopped in the kitchen. A cook was tending an oven, two men worked at K.P., another was cleaning a steam table.

"Get out of here," Colonel Vincent said. "And stay out till you hear from me."

The kitchen crew left without a word. Colonel Vincent pulled up chairs for the distad and himself, and they sat at a table covered with the beginnings of supper.

"Cornbread?" he asked. "They bake their own, every day."

"Sure," Dunbar said.

Colonel Vincent cut three or four slices and attempted to butter them. He failed. The bread, still warm and soft, crumbled beneath hard cubes of butter.

"Christ!" Colonel Vincent burst out, throwing the knife across the room. "Can't just one thing go right?"

"What's wrong?" Dunbar asked.

"This damn butter. They keep it in the fucking deep freeze! Throw this, you could put somebody's eye out!"

"I mean, what's the problem down here. Why'd you send for me?"

"You'll pass on the cornbread?"

"For now."

"All right," said Colonel Vincent. He swept aside the plateful of mashed crumbs and icy butter. "We killed a man on Peleliu. In the caves."

"I hear."

"Do you hear *whom* we killed?"

"No."

"Well, we don't know. That's the problem."
"You want me to identify him? That it?"
"Right."
"Where are you keeping him?"

Vincent motioned toward a massive metal door set into the wall on one side of the room.

"In the reefer there. The freezer section's through another door inside, on the left."

"What are you saving him for, Colonel? A taxidermist?"

Among the Coast Guard's steaks and chops and chicken, strawberry ice cream and french fries, lay the dead Palauan. Surrounded by alien provisions, he seemed local and inferior. And dirty. The mud which covered him in the cave had dried and caked. And then it had frozen.

"Some fudgesickle," Dunbar said grimly as he moved around the dead man's body to have a good look at his face. He stared at the dead man. He already knew, he had known right away, but he wanted to be absolutely sure. The short, heavy build. The dark skin. The coarse features. He was absolutely sure.

"What are you going to do with him?"
"We haven't decided. Maybe send him to Guam for disposal."
"You do that."
"Well . . . who is he?"
"I really can't say," the distad lied.
"A Palauan?"
"Probably. But nobody important." His second lie.
"Will he be missed?"
"Hard to say. If I get any reports on lost fishermen, it may give us a clue as to who he was. Meanwhile, I suggest you ship him out of here."

"He killed one of my men!"

"And he got killed by one of your men."

"He started it!"

"No. It's not like that. This guy didn't go to Guam. You came to Peleliu."

"He could have killed Elwell," the Colonel pleaded. "He could have been in on that!"

"Sure. Or he might have been stripping scrap around the caves when he saw a few hundred marines advancing at him with guns in their hands," Dunbar said. "No, just get his ass out of here. We'll hope his relatives assume he got lost fishing outside the reef."

"We could rig up a fishing accident," the colonel suggested. "Drop him outside the reef and let him float. Would that help?"

Dunbar had examined the man's head closely enough to recognize him. It was not hard. He had known him on and off for years, even briefly employed him as a manual laborer in the district Public Works Department. He glanced at the man's feet—the thickly callused soles; the wider-than-normal notch between toes, made by the rubber-thonged zoris he'd worn most of his life; the mosquito scars up and down his legs. Now he gestured at the middle of the man's body, at his splintered ribs, at red craters ripped into his abdomen.

"Some fishing accident that would be," the distad said. "Do tuna carry machine guns?"

"If you knew who the dead man was, why didn't you tell the colonel?" Beckman asked, interrupting the distad's story for the second time.

The question puzzled Booker. It was too nonchalant, too low-key. It was the second question, and nobody had asked the first one yet.

"Who *was* the dead man?" he interrupted.

Dunbar raised his tired head and looked Beckman straight in the eyes.

"Mo Kintaro."

"Any relation of . . . ?"

"His brother."

The distad let Beckman and Booker mull it over, just as he had on the boat back to Koror. He remembered Kintaro at the high school commencement, capitalizing on Elwell's death, rallying emotions against American presence on Peleliu, pumping hate and grievance and purpose into what had been a bookish, forlorn independence movement.

But there was more. Dunbar had known Francisco Kintaro for twenty years. He had watched the slow blending of native Palauan pragmatism, low-caste strivings, a brown man's distrust of whites, a colonial's distaste for his colonizers. He had seen how the last few years in Hawaii had added to all this the Third World's love of rhetoric and symbols. Kintaro had left for Hawaii an eager-to-please scholarship student; he had returned an avowed rebel.

Then, too, there was the relationship between the golden, gifted Francisco and his brawny, brawling, none-too-bright brother, Mo. That famous night at the Boom Boom Room when Francisco Kintaro had tested his tongue against a crew of Coast Guardsmen off a survey ship. *Why are you in Palau? Did any Palauans ask you to survey our harbors? Our fishing boats do not need surveys to cross the reef, but your warships do. What are you doing in the Boom Boom Room? Looking for Palauan girls? Are you out to screw my sisters? You think we are niggers?*

When the fight broke out, the scholarship winner had stepped aside, and it had been brother Mo who took on the Coast Guard, who collected the bruises, the cuts, the broken teeth.

Francisco had used his brother again and again. And now, thought Dunbar, he had used him once again. Used him up.

"You figure he got his brother to do it?" Booker asked. "Murder Elwell so he could exploit the flap?"

"Who else profited?" asked the distad. "Who else figured to gain?"

"That's really grim," Beckman said. "Sacrifice his brother to make a political point!"

"He didn't know Mo would get killed," the distad said. "No one expected Atkinson and his gang to chase him into his caves."

"So you busted Kintaro on suspicion?"

It had not been that simple, the distad replied. He had not been that brave. Back in Koror, he had thought it through, waffling, hesitating, until all his instincts, all his evidence, pointed him toward Kintaro.

Everywhere in Palau, there were signs of the unrest Kintaro had kindled. Tentative stirrings of anti-Americanism, a long-passive island people awakening into hate.

The first converts were the punks—the teen-age alcoholics who loafed around bars, fed on movies, and lip-read comic books. They had picked up Kintaro's slogan, "Elwell Was the Last." They lettered it on signs, shouted it at night as they zoomed through the government housing area on motorcycles.

But the punks were easy. They could be had by anyone who could promise them a spiffy uniform or a new guitar. Much more unsettling were the ripples of resentment that were spreading to the older Palauans. Dunbar's gardener spoke rudimentary English. Now he reverted to pure Palauan. Sick calls in government offices increased, and when Dunbar glimpsed the invalids in bars, they no longer ducked out of sight. They remained where they were, leaning against pool tables, staring back at him.

The surest sign of bad times came from the Peace Corps. Living among Palauans, the volunteers were more vulnerable than the other Americans. A volunteer teacher at Halsey High School reported that his classroom had been pillaged by a crew of dropouts. A Peace Corps girl was molested.

"Did you accuse Kintaro of conspiracy to murder Elwell?" Booker asked.

"No."

"Did you tell him about his brother?" asked Beckman.

"No. I thought I'd save that."

"Well, what the hell did you tell him?"

"Only that I suspected him."

"And you threw him into jail for being under suspicion."

"No," Dunbar said, "he threw himself into jail."

Though his home island was Peleliu, Francisco Kintaro used a residence in Koror. The place was on a narrow road called Geisha Lane. It had been lined with bordellos in Japanese times, and all the Palauan houses were perched on concrete slabs marking the ruins of larger Japanese structures. Kintaro's house was a little bigger than the others along Geisha Lane, but no better —wood and concrete meeting haphazardly under a metal roof. Around the house was the usual array of cooking sheds, washstands, outbuildings, water catchments. Palauans did not live in houses, they lived around them. The yard was full of people—women bringing in taro and tapioca, men mending fishnets or tinkering with engines, drinking beer or chewing betel nut.

Dunbar spotted Kintaro immediately. He was sitting on a rattan mat under a tree, a book at his side.

Kintaro waved to the distad. Not a wave of hello so much as a signal. Here I am, look no further, I'm not running away from you.

Dunbar walked toward him. The washing, the cooking, the tinkering, everything stopped. The chatter and the laughter, too. Only the drone of radios filled the air, and they were so common in Palau that it was less a noise than a part of the silence.

For a second, Dunbar wondered if Kintaro was up to an ambush—a symbolic stoning of the colonial administrator to follow the symbolic slaying of the marine war hero.

"Good afternoon, Francisco," the distad began. He was not sure about using the first name.

"What brings you here?" Kintaro asked. The book was *The Wretched of the Earth*.

"It has come to my attention that . . ."

"So formal?"

No one but Dunbar could hear Kintaro's laughter. From across the street, it looked like the visiting American was talking down to the Palauan, stepping onto his property, wrecking his peaceful afternoon.

". . . come to my attention that there may be reason to suspect your involvement in the death of Elwell. I came to tell you."

"What is the 'it'?" Kintaro asked.

"The what?"

"You know, the antecedent. The 'it' that has come to your attention?"

"Evidence. Linking you to the murder."

"What evidence?"

"I can't tell you," the distad said. "I'm not sure I should even be here. But I thought you should know."

Kintaro rose to his feet.

"I knew it," he said. "I always knew it. I'll pack my things."

"What for?" the distad asked. "Where are we going?"

"To jail. Aren't we?"

"That's not necessary," Dunbar replied. "Not in Palau. You haven't been convicted. You haven't even been charged. I was only informing you. Just don't leave the island."

"Don't run away and hide?" Kintaro shouted. "You come to my house and call me a murderer! You try to do it in a nice way! Informally! Well, I want my people to know what you've said! I want them to hear that I'm in jail! And that *you* put me there!"

Not only did Dunbar bear the full force of Kintaro's anger, he then had to endure more—Kintaro translated his shouting into Palauan!

"You accuse me of murder, then ask me to sit home and wait for my doom! Who will it be? Marines from Peleliu? Assassins of the C.I.A.? I insist on jail!"

"All right," said Dunbar after Kintaro had completed his second translation. "To jail."

Kintaro quieted down right away.

"Just a second," he whispered. "I'll throw some things in a bag."

That went untranslated.

Kintaro disappeared into the house. Everyone and everything else remained motionless—his family, his neighbors, the traffic along Geisha Lane.

Someday there may be paintings of this scene, Dunbar thought. Lurid, realistic murals depicting "The Arrest of the Leader." They'll hang it in the post office. If they have a post office.

Kintaro emerged carrying a Pan Am flight bag. They walked toward the distad's car. Dunbar opened the front door for him. Kintaro shook his head and opened the back door and got in.

Dunbar walked around to the front of the car, placed his hand on the door, and stepped back in alarm.

"Shit," he said.

The car was listing to one side. Two tires had been slashed.

"What now?" Kintaro asked.

"We can walk it," Dunbar said.

Kintaro frowned. Send me to jail, his expression said, but don't make me walk a mile in this heat!

He pointed to a Datsun parked at the side of his house.

"I'll drive," he said. "And *you* sit in the back."

The word had spread quickly. Geisha Lane was lined with people. A gang of dogs and children easily kept pace with the Datsun.

"I've lost count," Kintaro said. "How many years have you been in Palau?"

It was as though he had never shouted at Dunbar. At a distance, or in front of a crowd, Kintaro could be hostile. Up close, he was easy to get along with. Almost friendly.

"Twenty years," Dunbar answered.

"That long?" Kintaro said. "Well, now you're going to see what twenty years were worth."

The Koror jail was a joke, a collection of sheds set inside a rusty fence. The inmate population consisted of a half dozen long-term felons and a transient crew of drunks and juveniles. The permanent residents worked on handicrafts, cheerfully chipping away at story boards and tortoise-shell jewelry. They had turned the place into a minor tourist attraction. The younger prisoners went out armed with machetes, slapping at weeds along the roads and around public buildings. Between them—the wood carvers and weed choppers—they could have conquered Palau.

The police ran a sloppy, leisurely operation. Some invariably were related to the prisoners. Kinfolk brought food and visited throughout the day. At night, Dunbar knew, there was plenty of beer and whiskey. And conjugal privileges.

Kintaro parked in front and waved at a group of cops and prisoners chewing betel nut in the shade of the front porch. Kintaro got out of the car, walked toward them, and plopped down on the cool concrete. That was the beginning of his imprisonment.

Dunbar entered the jail to explain things to the deputy sheriff, fill out forms, and ask him to retrieve his car. When he left, Kintaro was still outside, smiling.

Across the street, a crowd had begun to gather. The punks arrived first. The first wholly American-educated generation of Palauans. The distad could count their motorcycles.

He walked home. It took twenty minutes. That was all the time they needed. To topple the birdbath and slash the porch screens. To empty and overturn the refrigerator. To shit on the mattress in the bedroom. To leave in haste. They left his valuable handicrafts collection undisturbed, but stole a case of beer.

Dunbar slept alone that night, dressed in clothes, stretched out on the living-room couch. Sleep came hard. He remembered Red Elwell, whose last nights had also been racked by insomnia.

Toward dawn, he paced the lawn in back of his home. The Japanese administrator who had ruled Palau before him had also liked the view from the hill, and had put his house on this same ridge. At the edge of the yard, the Japanese had built an outdoor bathing pool, tile-bottomed. Dunbar sometimes felt close to his unknown predecessor. Once he had promised himself that he would repair his pool and restore his gardens, now a ragged alcove of ferns and shrubs. A lot of vows had been made when he and his wife came bursting into the islands two decades before. They would restore baths, build greenhouses, tear a skylight in the roof, plow up a garden and screen it off to protect plants against snails.

There were other projects he remembered: they would commission a hand-hewn boat from the last surviving native craftsmen; they would establish a weekend bungalow on the northernmost atoll, Kayangel. And the biggest project of all: a new wing on their house, to be offered to creative visitors, invited at random from the outside world. One night, after playing *Carmina Burana,* Dunbar and his wife had started a letter to Carl Orff, beckoning the composer to six months' food and lodging and leisure on their islands.

Now, the distad saw, there was no boat, no skylight, no garden. The Japanese pool was cracked and buckling. Snails covered his sidewalk every morning. His first wife was gone, his second wife was absent, and he again felt close to the Japanese man who had lived on this ridge before him. Had he, too, loved the years when Palau was at the end of the world and he had it to himself? Had he sat night after night outside his home on the hill high above the sea, seeing his house flushed with gold, orange, and deep purple, the last place to sink into blackness, and felt himself a keeper of the islands? Had he, too, foreseen and dreaded the loss of it all?

III

"As a story, it ain't bad," Booker said later that night. "It's even persuasive. Kintaro's a bad-ass. I heard his speech at the high school. And I talked to him later that night at the Darling Bar."

"You think he set it up pretty much the way Dunbar described it?" Beckman asked.

They had left the distad and driven to the Royal Palauan Hotel, drinking in the lobby while Inez rested in her room. The barmaid sat in a chair nearby, eating a Cadbury's chocolate bar. Kintaro's jailing had been bad for business.

"Who else could have done it?" Booker said. "We're through with the Japanese, right? That leaves the Palauans. And, of the Palauans, Kintaro had the best motive. And his brother down there in the caves—that's really something."

"It rounds out your story."

"Nicely. From stragglers to bone hunters to natives. I can practically tell it the way it happened."

"I should be so lucky."

"Why?"

"Look, Kintaro is the man, okay? You know it and I know it. He found out Elwell was here and decided to stage some guerrilla theater. That's a good story. A hell of a story. But we can't convict him on that kind of evidence."

"Can't prove conspiracy?"

"We haven't got a prayer! Hell, I'm not sure we could have even convicted his brother, if he had lived, let alone pin something on Francisco. Kintaro can claim his brother was an innocent victim—that's his first line of defense. Then, he can claim that he had nothing to do with his brother—that's the second line. Last, he can claim that the whole thing is a frame set up to deflower his independence movement."

"You need his confession," Booker said.

"I need a miracle."

"Maybe we can't convict him," Booker said. "But we can still break him."

"What do you mean?"

Booker smiled. What a pleasure to be one step ahead of Beckman, to reach up and snap on a switch and stand back while he blinked in the light. For the first time since Tinian, they were going to be on equal ground again.

"The press," he said. "As in 'power of.' By the time I finish this story, Kintaro will be so covered with circumstantial shit, he couldn't be elected congressman from the Galapagos."

"You've got enough to do that?"

"I've got plenty."

"Even though it couldn't stand up in court?"

"Journalists don't need legal proof," Booker instructed. "All they need is a certain pattern of events. Enough to let the reader draw his own conclusions."

"I hadn't thought of that."

"The hell you hadn't." Booker was still a step ahead. "You sure as hell had thought about it. That's why you brought me down here again. That's why you made it easy for me and my lady to come. You knew that you wouldn't have enough to nail Kintaro. You brought me down so I could nail him for you. You must really want that sonofabitch."

"You're right," he said. "I do. Wouldn't you?"

"I'll do it," Booker said. "But it's going to cost you."

"What do you want?"

"I want a shot at that My Lai outfit," Booker said. "The whole sick, weird unit. I want the story."

"That'll be tricky."

"Think about it," Booker said. He stood up, ready to leave. Beckman remained seated, scratching the paper label off a Kirin bottle. Little strips of paper curled under his fingernails like pieces of skin.

"I have thought about it," Beckman said. "You're some smart guy."

"So?"

"You got yourself a deal."

IV

That night, Booker surprised Inez with his ardor. He was elated by the prospect of two sensational stories. More than that, he was pleased that he had won from Beckman something Beckman was reluctant to give. Now, it was he who moved and penetrated. And though it was Inez who struggled beneath him, moving all her wares and trickery, Booker thought that somewhere below Inez, deeper than sex, he could feel Beckman thrashing, too.

EIGHT
DO YOU BELIEVE IN LOVE?

I

Rampaging across the Pacific, a legendary giant had tripped over a reef, fallen, and died. His shattered body formed the islands of Palau. Where his head had landed, a high-caste village flourished. Where his genitals fell lay a low, rainy, mangrove swamp. His muscled torso was rolling Babelthuap, largest island of the group. And the little parts of his body, hundreds of tiny fragments, made up Palau's Rock Islands.

Not long after dawn, a small boat wound southward through these islands. As the boatman picked his way through the labyrinth of islands and channels, moving down alleys of clear water, Marshall Booker and his lady gazed up at the dozens of islands passing them on either side.

Up close, the Rock Islands were formidable. Booker saw piles of sheer limestone, shaped like giant mushrooms, slowly being undercut by the sea. The sides of the islands were steep and thickly forested, with pigeons darting among trees and vines. Many of the islands seemed almost untouchable—no beaches, no piers, no trails, no landings, no reason to land.

All the islands were uninhabited, except on weekends, when people came down from Koror to picnic, fish, or poach. A few of the islands had beaches, tiny white-sand coves. It was to the prettiest of these islands, Ulong, that Marshall Booker and Inez were bound.

The outing was Beckman's idea. He still wanted to try for a confession from Kintaro, although his chances were almost nil. While Beckman haggled in the jail, Booker and Inez would revel on Ulong. Later, Beckman would join them.

Booker leaped at the suggestion. He could not accompany Beckman to the jail, and he did not want to be pent up in the hotel. After a day or two, Koror was a stunningly dull town, a dusty, ramshackle rattletrap. It was sappingly humid during the day, and, at night, only bars relieved the tedium. With Inez at his service, Booker had better company than the bars could provide.

Inez smiled from beneath a straw hat she had bought the night before. Unaccountably, the store had not had proper wide-brimmed sun hats, so she had settled for a kind of baseball cap several sizes too large; as a result, she looked like an oversexed Little Leaguer. She wore shorts, rubber zoris, and an old blue shirt she had rooted out of Booker's luggage.

He liked having her wear his things. It meant that they were settling into a relationship. There were other signs of this. Their sex had grown more relaxed. They no longer felt they had to accomplish everything in one night, or every night, Booker heaving and sweating to get his money's worth, Inez remaining one trick ahead of him at all times. That sort of role-playing was over. Sex remained a constant, of course, but they were screwing each other a little less and—Booker thought —enjoying themselves a little more.

Now he would have a couple of days alone with her

before Beckman arrived. Time to pop the question, build confidence, allay doubts. Time enough, he hoped, to turn Inez into a New Yorker.

Before returning to Koror—where he would wait for Beckman—the boatman gave them a tour of the island. It did not take long. Ulong offered a tiny beach, fringed by palms and soft-needled pines. Behind the beach and at both sides of it towered rocky cliffs choked with brush and vines. To the southward side was the lagoon.

Off the beach was a shelter built on stilts, tin-roofed and open at the sides to catch the breeze coming in off the sea. In back were a water catchment and a small refrigerator, generator-powered.

The boatman helped Inez unpack, started the generator, checked the screens on top of the catchment barrels. It amused Booker to see how Inez set up housekeeping, ordering the man around. The sleeping mats went to the front of the platform—that was the bedroom. The Coleman stove had to be next to the refrigerator, and towels were to be stacked next to the catchment in the bathroom. Finally, Inez put two rolls of toilet paper in the boatman's hand and dispatched him down a trail to where toilets had been dug at the base of the cliff.

Booker was anxious to have the Palauan leave so they could doff clothing and claim the island as their own. But as soon as he came back, the boatman strapped on some goggles, grabbed a spear gun, and stepped out to the lagoon. Inez might think the world of Marshall Booker, but she clearly did not want to count on his underwater hunting for their supply of fresh fish.

Booker strode down to the edge of the water and watched the Palauan work. It could hardly be called fishing. He dove in and out of the water, and almost every time he surfaced, another fish was writhing on the end of his spear. Soon the floor of the boat was covered with fish—red snappers, a parrot fish, tuna, needlefish, and a half dozen small, bright reef fish Booker could not name.

After fifteen minutes, the Palauan swam down the beach to where limestone cliffs tumbled down to the sea. There he disappeared. Ten minutes later, he was back with four langusta on his spear.

Back at the boat, the Palauan worked quickly. While a tuna still quivered and fought for air on the fiberglass deck, the Palauan slashed part of its flank into bite-size slivers of sashimi. Next, he scaled, boned, and cleaned the other fish. Handfuls of guts went flying out over the lagoon, circled by a flock of birds.

When the Palauan left, Booker was elated. He and Inez now had the place to themselves. He threw his clothing against a palm trunk. He sprinted into the lagoon, splashing himself, displaying his body to the whole world. Then he walked slowly back to the hut, wanting Inez.

He stopped and frowned. She was not there. Uncertain, he stepped down the trail to the toilets. The rolls of paper were there, but Inez was not. Feeling foolish in his nakedness, Booker walked back to the beach. He scanned the white curve of sand, and all he saw was some birds diving for the last of the fish gore and entrails.

Then he froze in disbelief. An apparition had stepped out from behind a palm at the corner of the beach, and Booker knew he would remember this for the rest of his life. He would be a dried-up old man sitting in a rocker on the veranda of the old folks' home, drooling spit and memories, missing his prostate gland, and he would recall what he saw now. Every sense diminished and near death, he would die with a clear picture of Inez, standing on the beach of their private island, brown and naked and laughing.

She pointed at him from where she stood, smiled, and sprinted down the beach, daring him to catch her.

Booker shouted with pleasure and set out in pursuit. The island girl ran at least as well as he did. Her bobbing breasts slowed her down, but she was lean and trim below the waist and set a respectable pace up and down the beach, in and out of the water, dodging and evading her lunging, tiring lover.

He might never have caught her if she had not turned to laugh at him, at his patchy, irregular tan, and if she had not come to a spot, a shady green place, where she wanted to be caught.

II

In the late afternoon the sun weakened, the heat passed, and they could come out of the shade and walk the beach together. The harsh midday light vanished, and nuances of color returned to the island—oranges, yellows, and pinks—along with a mellow feeling carried on the breeze.

Inez knelt down at the very edge of the beach and began running her fingers through the sand. Pleased, she held up a tiny green-tinted shellfish, no larger than her thumbnail. She kept working her hands in the sand, and each time she came up with three or four of them. She told Booker they were fine for soup but they would need lots of them. So he sat beside her, helping.

He was concerned with her being a whore. Marshall Booker knew enough to laugh at boyish visions of prostitutes with hearts of gold. Thinking about Inez in New York, he worried that the whorishness would come out in her—streaks of cheapness, avarice, vulgarity. Now, at the edge of the beach, his worries lifted. On this island, Inez became an island girl, reverting to her origins, as if she had never lived—or worked—on godawful Guam. She was not a prostitute, not at heart. Born on some sleepy sandpile at the end of the world, she had been surrounded by a society of men who gathered scrap metal and fished, who drank too much and grew fat young. Fleeing a world of minor league machismo, she came to Guam. Guam was freedom. Prostitution was the price of freedom, her only way out of a life of annual child-bearing and endless dullness. She was no more a whore than the Tahitian girls who had swarmed over the ships of Captain Cook, gladly giving themselves for some iron nails or a bolt of cloth, for the artifacts, for the very glimpse of a new world.

He asked her that night, after they had eaten. Inez was sitting on the platform, dangling her legs over the side. It was cooler now, and she was wearing shorts she had manufactured by chopping up a pair of Booker's denims. She was playing with the radio. During the day, there was only one station up and down the band, the government broadcast from Koror. But at night, you could pick up stations from the Philippines and Japan, eerie waves of words and music, now close, now far away, like transmissions from the bottom of the ocean.

Booker sat down beside her. She immediately smiled and sidled against him, her hand moving over his leg. He turned to face her, propping his hand under her chin. A serious discussion, this was going to be.

"It's nice here," he began. "It's almost nicer than any place I've ever been."

She nodded, agreeably enough.

"We're—what?—ten miles away from the nearest people. We're twenty miles away from the nearest town. Eight hundred miles away from the nearest city, the nearest factory, the nearest smokestack. The rest of the world—it's as far away as those stations we hear on the radio at night."

He spoke slowly, pronouncing every word, careful not to risk an expression, an idiom, an irony she could not grasp.

"For me, living in New York, it's wonderful to come to an island like this," he continued. "And I'll remember it. Wherever I am, just knowing that this place is here will make me feel good."

So far, so good, Booker thought. She's with me.

"But you can't lie on a beach forever, Inez. You would not want to spend the rest of your life here. It would get . . . boring."

She nodded.

"We go back to Guam!" she said decisively. Booker felt that he had only to say the word and she would start to break camp, trading paradise for a military base. But he had to be patient. Guam was all she knew.

"We'll go back to Guam in a few days," he agreed. "Then I will leave for the United States. And I want you to come with me."

She did not get proposals like this every day. Did she? And yet, she did not react.

"You understand, Inez? I want you to come with me to New York. We'll live together. For as long as you like it. I want you to like it. I want you to stay for a long time. But if you get tired, you can go back."

"You'll take care of me?" she asked in a low voice.

"I'll take care of you, no matter what," he affirmed.

"How long we'll stay in New York?" she asked.

"As long as you want to."

She thought it over for a moment. Booker tried to imagine the multitude of doubts and questions that must be attacking her now, and braced himself to answer all of them. When he tried to see it through her eyes, he was appalled at the enormity of the change he had proposed.

"Okay," she said. "I'll go with."

"You will?" he said. He was startled. Just like that? No questions about the city, about racial attitudes in the States, about crime or pollution or snow? About money? Was this their courtship?

"Okay," she chirped. Then—after a pause—the first afterthought crossed her face.

"Can we stop in Hawaii? To see my sister? We can stay with her."

"Sure we can!" he responded, amazed that it was all going to be that simple.

That night, while they played cards, Inez was more talkative than ever before. She told Booker about Ponape, her mother's island, about deer that ran through mountain rain forests, about rickety wooden bridges over jungle streams where women washed clothes on flat rocks, about mile-deep mangrove swamps. She talked about deaths, and feasts, and ghosts, and rebellions that went back to German times, all the lore of the islands she was leaving.

III

Sleep, that night, was more than mere rest. They lay on mats at the front of the platform. They felt long, steady breezes play over their bodies. They heard the mild slap of waves against the beach, the rustling of palm branch against palm branch, the sounds of night birds up on the cliffs. Sleeping, they did not shut out the world, bundle themselves away from it. They were part of it, and it conspired to give them pleasure.

Until the mood was broken.

Booker heard it first—a dissonant noise in the night—the sound of a machine coughing in the water, an outboard motor at its lowest and quietest.

He sat up and looked out at the beach.

They were no longer alone on their island. Someone else had come to visit.

A boat sat quietly offshore, hardly moving. Three figures sat inside, hardly moving. One of them was at the back, in control of the outboard. The other two held flashlights over the gunwales, like they were looking for something on the bottom of the lagoon. It was hard to see much of them. Nothing betrayed their identity or purpose, but Booker shuddered as he recalled Atkinson's tale of how men with flashlights had surrounded Elwell in the jeep.

The flashlights scared him. The men scared him. He felt vulnerable, camped out on an island without a boat, without a weapon, the island hardly large enough to hide on, the surrounding sea preventing an escape. It had seemed so secure, so romantic, their place to swim and go naked.

He found a flashlight, climbed down from the platform, and moved slowly toward the beach. He took a circular route, from tree to tree. He needed several minutes to work his way down to the edge of the water, but he was confident that no one in the boat could tell where he was standing.

If the men in the boat were enemies, the time to find out was while they were still offshore. It would take them time to clamber over the side, to walk in to the beach. He and Inez could use those moments to advantage.

Booker stood and watched. The motors were still idling, but the boat had not moved, nor the men who were in it. The next move was up to Booker.

He took the flashlight in both hands, held it at arm's length, and pointed it straight out toward the strangers. His thumb crept toward the switch and slid it forward, to the "on" position.

A powerful beam shot across the cove and hit square against the boat. And lit up a still-life.

It was a good-sized fiberglass runabout, lime-green, twelve or fifteen feet long, with a couple of outboards hitched onto the back.

The men were dressed in a black plastic material, something like a cheap rain slicker. All Booker could see were their backs and their shoulders. They kept their faces turned away from him, and the two men in front still held flashlights over the side. As yet, no one had stirred. It was as if they were playing that childhood game where someone shouts "freeze" and everyone remains in a fixed position; whoever moves first loses. For at least thirty seconds, Booker held them like that in the beam of his flashlight.

When action came, it came in a rush. As if on cue, the two men who held flashlights raised up their beams and aimed at Booker. Now a bright alley of light connected the journalist and his visitors.

At the same time, the third man reached down to the floor of the boat, and it looked as if he were unwrapping something—a flashlight of his own, perhaps—lifting it, pointing it. A gun.

Now it was Booker's turn to freeze, to squint, to stand transfixed. When movement came, it was only because he had been hit, tackled, knocked off balance onto the ground, his flashlight sent spinning into the water.

"Inez!"

"They have a gun."

They had rolled behind a stand of soft-needled pine and lay together on the ground, looking out through the screen of trees. The lights in the boat had gone out. The three shadowy figures leaned toward each other, consulting. Then came the sound of the outboard churning the water. Slowly—they were in no rush to flee—the boat turned and moved away from the island.

Standing up, Booker moved forward to watch the boat putt-putting away, the three men facing out toward the sea, still and dark, like figures in mourning. They rounded the corner of the island and vanished.

"Who were they?" Booker asked. "What did they want?"

"I don't know," Inez said. "I followed you to the beach, but I stay in the trees. I had fear. When I saw the man lift his gun at you . . ."

"You saved my ass. I never thought he would have a gun! Could you tell how dark . . . if they were Palauans?"

"No," she said. "They were dressed in dark, and their faces they turned away."

"They never even spoke. Not a word. What did they want?"

"I think . . ." Inez began tentatively.

"What?"

"Sometimes people come to these island at night to take turtle. And turtle egg. The law says no. So they come at night."

"Poachers?"

"I don't know that word."

"Never mind. Are the people who poach . . . the people who take the turtles . . . are they Palauans?"

"Yes," she said. "Sometimes. But Japanese and Okinawan, too. They fish outside the reef. The law says they cannot land. So they come in at night."

"They expected the island to be empty," Booker said, retrieving his flashlight from the water.

"They maybe thought you were from island police," Inez said.

"Sure," Booker said. "Out defending the turtles."

They walked back to the platform, Inez holding on to him. He doubted they would fall asleep again that night. He reached his arm around the girl and laughed. Topless, she had come to the rescue.

IV

Late the next morning, Booker and Inez went swimming. With Beckman expected at any time, this was their last chance for a nude swim in the lagoon. Booker insisted they leave their things on a blanket on the beach, and Inez did not protest. They entered the water with nothing more than a pair of snorkels and a spear gun.

They spent an hour diving and exploring. Inez laughed while Booker ineffectually hunted and missed dozens of gorgeous fish. She swam better than he, moved faster, dove deeper, stayed down longer, burst out of the water to tease him after every miss. The more Booker practiced with the spear gun, the wider were his errors, and the greater Inez's amusement. Finally, Booker was so anxious to prove himself that he rushed reloading. When he shot, the spear plopped listlessly into the water and sank at his feet.

That was too much for Inez. Laughing until tears came, she held Booker in the water. They embraced, standing on the white sand at the shallow side of the fringing reef. When her fit of laughter had subsided, Inez teased him affectionately, holding him close, whispering a clear sexual challenge, something to the effect that she hoped his loving was better than his spearfishing, or she would have to swim to another island and find a man who was more accurate with his weapon.

Booker took up her dare, glad at the chance to recoup his pride. He had never made love in the water, not outside a bathtub, but now he supposed it was possible. He slid his hands down her back, pulled her close, then hoisted her up, so that her thighs spread around his middle and her legs wound and met in back of him. The water made her light and buoyant, and she began moving up and down, as if rocked by the waves.

Booker held her, forced her against him. He faced away from the island, looking out at the sea. There was lively hunting underwater.

He felt Inez's hands moving up and down his back, felt her nails scratching. He closed his eyes and aligned himself for the last thrust. Then her nails dug deeper, flaying his back. It hurt, too much.

"Inez, not so much," he gasped, opening his eyes.

That was when he saw on her face what her hands had tried to communicate: not ecstasy, but fear. Panicked, she looked past him, over his shoulders, in at the island, at the two men who had captured the beach behind them.

There was no boat this time. Booker guessed that they had walked around from the other side of the island. And he was sure that the two men were part of the group he had seen the night before. Their movements were slow and deliberate, their features indistinct. And they still wore black rubbery garments.

Unable to poach, they had returned to steal. One of the men sauntered up to the beach house while his partner stayed behind.

"They only want our things," Booker whispered. "When they take what they want, they'll leave."

The man came back from the house, empty-handed. Joining his partner, they knelt down over the blanket of discarded clothing.

"Your wallet," Inez said.

"So what? Only sixty dollars and some credit cards."

But he was wrong again. The poachers did not linger over the blanket, did not pause to dig through the clothing. Instead, they looked out at the sea.

Booker and Inez ducked even farther down into the water, but they had to leave room to breathe, and their heads were clearly above the surface. The men on the beach scanned the lagoon, carefully scrutinizing the reef, whispering and gesturing. And then one of them, shading his eyes, pointed straight to where Booker and Inez were hiding.

"They see us!" she said.

"Hold on," Booker said. "We won't move till we're sure."

Then they were sure. One of the men opened a rectangular satchel and began fitting something together. So slow, so nonchalant were his motions, he might have been assembling a beach umbrella, not a rifle.

"They want us," Booker said. "We can't stay here."

They were a pair of naked swimmers, unarmed except for the spear gun Booker had toyed with. Against them were two men with a rifle. All that separated them was forty yards of warm water, hip-deep, covering a shelf of white sand. If they stayed where they were, they would be picked off in no time, shot from shore.

They would have to swim for it, swim outside the fringing reef, where the water was deeper, the waves choppier. They would swim underwater. But where to?

There was only one destination—the other side of the island. On one side of the beach, the cliffs left room for men to walk over coral. That was how the gunmen had come. The cliffs on the other side of the beach were another matter, plunging straight down into the sea.

The cliffs—and the converging currents which pounded against them—left no room to pass on land.

If they could swim there, around to the back of the island, they might be safe. The men on the beach had no boat. Most likely, they had left it on the other side, with the third member of their team to guard it. And if they swam in pursuit, they would have to leave their rifle behind.

Booker pointed out their destination. It was not inviting. The waves slammed against the rocks, filling the air with noise and spray, and there was no way of knowing whether the currents might pull them in, rubbing them against the sharp underwater coral, grating skin and flesh. And then, what about the other side of the island? What if there was no place to land, only more cliffs and waves and coral? Could they tread water until Beckman arrived?

They had no choice. The marksman on shore was damned slow—smug and confident—about screwing his machine together, but before long, he would surely be ready for the kill.

Booker explained it to Inez. They would swim underwater to the point; they would swim apart; they would space their trips to the surface at irregular intervals—twenty strokes and breathe, ten strokes and breathe, fifteen and breathe. They would leave their snorkels, which would betray their position, but Booker would carry the spear gun.

He made Inez go first although she was the better swimmer. Ten seconds after Inez left, Booker took a deep breath and followed.

Outside the reef, the water was rougher, colder, and deeper; the sand bottom dropped out of sight. Ahead of him, Inez moved rapidly through the water. After twenty strokes she surfaced, breathed, kept moving.

Now it was Booker's turn for air. He popped his head out of the water and filled his lungs. Looking back at the beach was a luxury he could not afford. Or resist. In the same instant he saw the men on the beach, they sighted him.

He ducked beneath the water again. He had expected to hear shots, but it was quiet underwater. Instead, he *saw* the bullets, saw them before he realized what they were, little furrows plowing into the water as if someone were skimming rocks, not spraying bullets.

He was tiring. After ten strokes, he needed to breathe again. When he surfaced, he stayed longer than he should have, exhausted, treading water. A sitting duck. The bullets were all around him, front and back. He was bracketed.

Booker pushed himself under and swam a mere ten feet. The marksman overestimated his swimming—the bullets moved off ten and twenty feet ahead. Fifty feet farther on was Inez, attracting no bullets. Slow-moving, out-of-breath Booker was the target.

He breathed again and looked back. The marksman had guessed that they were heading around the point. To keep his target in view, he had waded out into the water. They would have to swim completely around the point before they would be out of sight.

Nearer the point, the water grew turbulent. If Booker circled too close to the cape, he might be pulled in and pressed against the rocks. If he made a wide turn, he would prolong his exposure to the gunman. Inez made the decision for him. The wide turn.

Underwater, Booker shifted to a clumsy breast stroke. It was slow but steady, and it allowed him to regulate his breathing. He came to the surface more often, but he did not have to remain there as long.

Two worlds. Underwater, there was silence, green light turning cobalt blue in the depths. Above, a bowl of air, a brilliant sky, churning waves, sunlight, and the sound of shots echoing off the cliffs.

Twice more, Booker came up for air. Each time, a bullet came near his head. The marksman and he were both guessing at the same game. The man with the gun had learned to wait for Booker to come to the surface instead of plowing the sea for an underwater target.

So far, Booker had won, surfacing safely a half dozen times. But his luck could not continue forever. And the marksman only had to score once to end the match.

Sighting the edge of the point, Booker gulped and dove, swearing he would not breathe again until he was safe. He committed himself to fifteen strokes, then told himself he could do five more. His lungs protested, panic welled into his head, but he promised himself three more strokes, then just one. You can always do one more, one more won't kill you. He lost count, another stroke, one more, and then, no more. He popped out of the water and knew he was done swimming underwater forever.

Well ahead, Inez raised an arm out of calmer waters, waved hello. Behind him, Booker saw a wall of rock and spray. He had rounded the point.

V

If the south side of Ulong evoked Tahiti, the north side suggested Nova Scotia—a twelve-foot wall of grim rock cut and chipped by an unfriendly sea. Only a few little notches and crevices had been chopped out of the limestone facade. The first of these was a hundred yards from the point. Booker pointed, and they swam in.

Winded, Booker clambered over a wet rock, crept over the water line, and stretched out on the floor of their refuge. It was nothing more than a niche, fifteen feet across, twenty feet deep. On both sides, rock walls prevented their looking up or down the coastline. Behind them was more rock, covered with vines and trees, the base of the ridge which formed the backbone of the island.

They sat down together, a pair of castaways. The bullets had missed, but not the coral. Coming in to shore, both of them had been cut, and their legs were covered with bleeding scratches which the flies were already discovering.

Inez leaned against him, relaxed. She picked bits of coral out of her legs, slapping salt water over the wounds.

"It's not over," Booker warned her.

She looked up in renewed alarm.

"We're not safe here," he said.

They were more vulnerable now than they had been on the beach or in the water, he explained. The attackers would pick up their gun and return to where they had spent the night on this side of the island, probably in a little cove like this. Then the three of them could hop into their boat and cruise along, checking out each little opening as they came to it. And when they passed by, they could hover offshore and shoot at will, kill without even landing. The same boat that brought the killers would carry them away. Unless Booker got to the boat and to the man who was guarding it first.

He could be anywhere along this half mile of eroding cliff, twenty feet or a half mile away, waiting for his companions to return from the pretty side of the island.

For the second time, Booker faced an unenviable choice. Land or sea?

Inez and he could swim from cove to cove, looking for the lime-green boat. They would make no noise that way, and they would not expose themselves as long as they stayed in the water. If discovered, they could dive and escape. Anyone who followed would have to take to the water, too.

But there were problems. The third man, the guardian of the boat, might be facing out to sea. Coming out of the water to attack, Booker would be in full view, awkward, slow, slipping over rocks, floundering for a foothold before he could reach for his spear gun and bring it to bear. And what if the third man was waiting in the boat itself, nestled against the idling outboards? What chance would they have against the boat?

No, they would have to go by land, climb up and mountain-goat their way along the ridge, moving slowly above the shoreline until they found the boat.

The back of the cove was steep, but there were plenty of crevices and outcroppings to climb on. The problem was their feet—every step over the coral opened new wounds or aggravated old ones. Not until they reached forty or fifty feet above the shoreline was the slope blanketed with leaves and soil. Here, things went easier, and they moved along briskly on a line above the beach, a brown-skinned Jane and an inept Tarzan.

In about two hundred yards, they passed three coves. Two were underwater, waves thundering in and out. The third cove, high and dry, was vacant.

Then came a hundred yards of even, unbroken shoreline. Near the center of the island, the wall of coastal rock grew higher, steeper, firmer. Booker began to doubt that there would be any more openings. They were nearing the end of the island when they found the last cove. It was a tiny harbor, barely large enough to nestle one lime-green boat.

They crept down the slope, squeezing between trees,

wincing as they stepped back onto the jagged coral. Finally they neared the edge of the little inlet. Not twenty-five feet away, the boat bobbed peacefully in protected waters. It was empty.

Booker lowered himself to his belly and wrapped an arm around a tree trunk to prevent himself from falling over the edge onto the little beach. Cautiously, he stuck his head over the side of the pit. If the third man were not in the boat, he would have to be at the back of the cove, against the wall.

He was. He was a light-brown-skinned man, dressed like his partners. Rubbery black shoes protected him against the coral. They matched his black swim trunks and black shirt. He was sitting against the wall, enjoying the shade, facing the sea. At first, Booker thought he might be dozing. Then he noticed the man held a lighted pipe in his hand. A contemplative man, he seemed, a pipe smoker, dreaming thoughtfully while his partners went out to kill. Some of the smoke drifted up Booker's way. It made him feel like a barbarian, a naked spear-carrier stalking the camp of a missionary explorer. Except that this missionary wore a holster with a pistol.

Booker rose to his feet and grasped the spear gun in his right hand. He brought his feet to the edge of the rim, as if he were on a diving board. He looked back at Inez, seeking an exchange of glances before the leap, but their eyes did not make contact. Her stare was already fastened on the pebbly beach, on what had not yet happened, on what would happen now.

Booker jumped. He landed upright, off balance, staggering to right himself. The guardian of the boat looked up in alarm, his seaside reveries at an end.

What did he make of what he saw? Of a naked white man dropping out of the air with a spear gun in his hand? Of a spear gun turning into a bayonet?

He rose and fumbled for his holster, but Booker was closing in on him. Giving up on his gun, the man bounded back toward the boat, but Booker adjusted and followed, all his weight behind the weapon.

At the edge of the water, by the side of the boat, he speared the man.

There was a gap between the rubber jacket and the rubber trunks, and here, in the midriff, the spear had plunged.

Booker held one end of the spear. The boatman held the other—in his stomach. They faced each other, Booker standing, his victim folding down onto his knees, as if the two of them were about to start a terribly unfair tug of war.

Booker saw the man's hand reach toward the holster, his fingers flicking pathetically at the button. Booker pressed down on the spear and another half inch of metal penetrated. The man flinched and screamed. His eyes pleaded for mercy. His hands obediently returned to the spear, both of them clutching the shaft where it had entered the stomach.

The man tugged at the spear, ineffectively struggling to pull it out, and it cost him another scream. Then he seemed to grow reconciled to the spear. His hands held onto it, almost in a caress. So long as it went no farther in, no farther out, he would settle for that. He could put up with dying that way, dying with his feet on land, his body in the water, his head against the boat, a slow, unspectacular trickle of blood around the edges of his wound.

"Take out the spear!"

Booker ignored the voice, remained standing, watching the man he had speared. The wound was surely mortal. Blood was coming out of his mouth now.

"Take the spear. Pull it!"

It was Inez, at the top of the rocks.

"Pull it!" she pleaded.

Booker grasped the end of the spear. But he made the mistake of looking back down at the man, of meeting his eyes. And Booker knew he would leave the spear.

"Pull the spear!" Inez repeated urgently. She pointed to the right, jabbing the air.

Booker stepped over his victim, waded past the boat, and looked around the limestone promontory. Before he could see what was there, an explosion in the wall, splintering dust and rock, told him. The other two had come, and they had brought their gun. The chance for escape over water was gone. In an open boat, they stood no chance against that gun.

He clambered back to Inez, and together they scrambled upward. There was no getting out of range before the two men entered the cove. But they could get under cover and hope. Running straight uphill, they plunged into the first rows of trees. Shots sounded behind them. They kept moving up the slope. Every trunk, every sapling, every leaf that screened them from down below was so much armor.

The men on the beach were firing rapidly, peppering the whole side of the ridge. Leaves and branches tumbled through the air, severed vines collapsed, bark shattered, flights of pigeons swarmed as shots came crashing into the foliage. The whole island seemed to tremble, rocks tumbling down past them, and Booker realized the men were throwing hand grenades.

Then, suddenly, it stopped. The men were done taking their revenge on the island, out of ammunition or out of anger. The battle was over.

The two men packed up quickly. They pulled out the

spear, with no qualms, no protest, no doubt about the third man's being dead. They loaded his body into the boat, face down, and threw the spear on top of it. They boarded the boat, steered it offshore, opened up both outboards, and raced over the lagoon. They headed straight across to the main reef, found a pass, turned south toward Angaur, and disappeared.

Bit by bit, Booker and Inez reclaimed the island. They walked the beach, stalked the trails, reentered the shelter. The mats, the supplies, their clothing, everything was as it had been. But everything had changed. Booker wanted to leave Ulong now, if he had to build a raft to do it.

They took everything they owned out of the shelter and carried it down to the beach. They filled the house with brush, weeds, palm fronds. Booker wanted lots of smoke. Then he splashed fuel oil all over their dream house.

The place exploded into flame, and a thick column of whitish smoke rose above the island. Together, they sat by their luggage and waited to see whom the bonfire would bring in off the darkening sea.

It was an old Palauan man and his boy in a decrepit wooden boat. Probably, they were poachers. In the back, under a bloody canvas tarp, were three suspiciously turtle-shaped humps.

The old man agreed to take Booker and Inez off the island. Not back to Koror. That was too far, and it was getting dark. He would take them to the nearest island of size, the nearest populated island.

That would be Peleliu.

NINE
DEAD HEAT

I

Atkinson's house made a pool of light in the dark Palauan village. Its yard was littered with empty beer cans and tins of corned beef. Hillbilly music sounded from inside. Approaching, Booker felt he was already safely at home in America.

Atkinson, of course, was drunk, entertaining a half dozen Coast Guardsmen from Angaur. Booker doubted that the demolitions chief made much sense of his account of what had happened on Ulong, or his request that Beckman be contacted by radio. But Atkinson did show them to his bedroom, a sanctuary of soiled sheets, brown pillowcases, dirty laundry, and a half dozen kinds of after-shave lotion on a cigarette-scarred dresser. Atkinson did not seem in the least surprised to see Marshall Booker again.

Inez fell asleep instantly, but Booker tossed and turned. He had killed a man, and the thought of it disgusted him. He felt revulsion at the memory of driving the spear into the man's midriff, of jabbing it in a half inch farther, of his victim's struggling against, then caressing, the instrument of his death.

From the next room, a shaft of light shone under the door, cigarette smoke and laughter blew on through, along with snatches of conversation from Atkinson's party. Oh, they were having a good time in there, trading memories of that satellite world of clubs and parlors, bars and spas, which had sprung up on the periphery of the American presence in Southeast Asia. He heard the conversation wander from Saigon to Taiwan to Subic Bay, from Bangkok to Okinawa to Manila. He heard talk of dance halls where girls rented by the weekend, baths where they hired out by twos or threes, bars where hostesses dipped under tables to perform fellatio, competing with each other for the highest daily score. Americans were getting around the world all right these days, good old boys spending time in some far places.

The noise dipped, the lights dimmed, and Booker thought the party was over, until he heard the whirring of a movie projector, laughs, and low whistles at Atkinson's blue movie. Finally, sleep crept up on Booker, and the last thing he heard was a drunken shout from one of the Coast Guardsmen.

"If you can't fuck 'em, kill 'em!" he shouted.

And an automatic response from the others.

"If you can't kill 'em, fuck em!"

II

"It's the damnedest thing," Merle Atkinson reflected. "In the morning, I'm always sober as a judge."

He leaned back in a chair that was propped against the front of his house, a beer and a cigarette his breakfast.

"No matter how late I'm up, how much I drink and

entertain, come mornin', I'm sittin' out here, feelin' okay. Not great, but okay."

"You gave us the master bedroom," Marshall Booker said.

"Master bedroom? Man, I live like a pig! Showing skin flicks at half a buck a head, Jap helmets for a door prize. Your woman inside?"

"Still sleeping. Did you remember to radio Beckman, tell him to pick us up here and not over on Ulong?"

"Been done. He said he's on his way, you shouldn't budge. I guess you had a real scare over there. You said they was poachers?"

"That's what Inez thought. They went to a hell of a lot of trouble for some turtle shells."

"They live like animals on those fishing boats, months at a time. Could be they wanted to hump your old lady." Atkinson raised his beer can and drank slowly, as if to say that you really could not blame the poachers for craving Inez. Yet there was something sad, vicarious, about his lust. Inez was out of Atkinson's class, and he knew it: she was a hundred dollar-an-hour model, and he was a hard-hat worker sitting on a sidewalk, eating lunch out of a pail. All he could offer was a whistle and a leer.

"I couldn't hang around Ulong after what happened there," Booker said. "I want to thank you for taking us in."

"It was nothing. Besides, I owed you."

"How's that?"

"That snapshot I gave you of Elwell and the bone hunters—I'll bet that didn't work out too good."

"No, Merle, matter of fact, it didn't. Damn, boy, you handed it to me like it was the map to buried treasure. When I caught up with those Japs on Tinian, one look told me you must've been drunk. It was like hunting for a rapist in an old folks' home."

"I got carried away," Atkinson admitted. "This thick hick skull of mine. I wasn't tryin' to send you off on no wild goose chase, though."

"Forget it. The guilty party's been nailed."

"Kintaro? I hear they locked him up."

"Yeah. The guy we found in the caves was his brother."

"And that wraps it up, huh?" Atkinson tossed his empty beer can into the yard. "Me and my big mouth. It gets me in trouble. And other folks, too."

"It's all right, Merle. You were drunk that night."

"But I'm sober now. And it's what I'm about to tell you that's worryin' me."

"You got *another* theory, Merle?"

"Why don't you just tell me to shut up? I'd appreciate it. It's not like you and me was bosom buddies or nothing."

"Oh, let's hear it, for the hell of it," Booker said. "Or let me guess. The Klan killed Elwell. No, make it the Peace Corps. They ambushed him. How about the Mafia?"

"You're gettin' warm."

"What?"

"Let's take a ride," Atkinson said. "I'm better at the showin' than the tellin'."

"What about Inez?"

"Leave her sleep. She don't want to go where we're goin'."

They entered the mountain through the same tunnel the marines had cleared for the final assault on the Japanese headquarters. Moving down the steps toward the crawlway, flashlights in front, Booker saw that there were no more Jap bodies on any of the landings. He did not ask where they'd gone. Atkinson was supposed to be doing him a favor this morning.

No one had disturbed things in the Japanese headquarters. As before, water dripped from the limestone ceilings onto broken desks and tables, piles of uniforms and guns and rations. Six inches of stagnant oily water covered the floor. With the prospect of stragglers permanently discredited, the place was more like a grave than ever. And the grave was still occupied.

"That's right," Atkinson confirmed. "They're all still here. Nobody's been foraging. I just been down a few times."

"Making an inventory?"

"Taking attendance, you could say. I'm gonna empty this place a little bit at a time."

"What'd you want to show me, Merle? It's not like I hadn't seen all this before."

"We both been here before, I know. Except neither of us was thinkin' at the time."

Atkinson sloshed across the floor to one of the crawlways.

"You remember this one?" he asked. "It's where Rivera got chopped up. And you remember when I found the plate in the wall outside, how it was all sealed and rusted over?"

"I sure do. We had to pry it open."

"Okay. Now, over there, you see the other crawlway. And that plate was rusted over, too, the same way, and the tunnel behind it was choked up besides. The marines had to dig their way in."

"Right again. So what?"

"Don't you see it? The Palauan guy—Kintaro's brother—couldn't come in through either of the two crawlways we know about. They were both closed up when we found 'em. So how did he get in? And if he got in some other way, why didn't he get out while the gettin' was good?"

"What'd you find Merle?"

"Look over here."

He led Booker over to the darkest, farthest corner of the cave, past a disorderly tangle of wooden sawhorses, broken masonry, steel reinforcing rods, and electrical wiring.

"All this was piled against the wall," Atkinson said. "I had to move it over."

There was another exit out of the headquarters, a third crawlway. Booker knelt down and stuck his flashlight into the hole.

"It's blocked up," he said.

"You bet it is. With dirt and rocks piled in from the other side, plus a few boulders. I found the tunnel leadin' into this crawlway, and there's a whole load of spade marks on the other side, where they shoveled the dirt in."

"What do you figure?"

"This is how they came in . . ."

"They?"

"I always said I saw three, four men around Elwell's body. This is how they got in. And this is how they got out. All except the brown man."

"They sealed him in? They wanted him to be found?"

"Right. They ditched the politician's brother."

III

They returned to the center of the room and sat on one of the Japanese worktables. They put out their flashlights and sat in the dark, listening to the water come down from the ceiling. It was almost like rain.

Merle Atkinson and Marshall Booker lit cigarettes and smoked in silence.

"I don't know, Merle," Booker said. "First, it was stragglers. But there are no stragglers. Then it was bone hunters—and they didn't work out. Then it was Kintaro and the Palauans."

"But Palauans wouldn't have left one of their own behind in here," Atkinson said. "It appears to me you're clear outta suspects, Mr. Booker."

"Can we finish thinking about this aboveground?"

"I ain't done yet," Atkinson said. He was sitting next to Booker, an indistinct figure, a face and a hand around a glowing cigarette. "Besides, I want to talk to you here, where it's dark and quiet. I can look at you this way and not see the look on your face. I'm starin' at you right now, Mr. Booker. Can you tell?"

"No. Make it fast, Merle. I'm not at home in caves."

"I want you to pretend you're just hearin' this, like from a man who was talkin' to hisself. Anybody asks, you just came down here on your own and found the tunnel, like a good reporter would. I wasn't nowhere around."

"Okay, Merle. As far as I'm concerned, you're home getting drunk right now."

"You know those Coast Guard fellas was at the house last night? They used to come over pretty regular. I'd set 'em up with some movies and beer, and maybe nookie, dependin' on what was available. If they wanted to buy some military souvenirs, that was gravy. Only I ain't seen 'em for a while, not for weeks—till last night. And I wondered whether I'd pissed somebody off and got my place declared off-limits. Well, the boys loosened up some—this was before you showed up—and let on that discipline's been pretty tight around the station lately. I ask why—it's only a long-range radio navigation station. And they tell me things got strange when they started gettin' off-schedule flights from Guam, carryin' special teams of guys who don't talk or mix much. Like they stick to theirselves, eat alone, all in one barracks. 'Cept when they took off in a boat around when Elwell was here, and come back a couple days later, lookin' bushed and dirty. So you figure it out."

"Americans?"

"Americans."

"Maybe they were part of Vincent's operation."

"They didn't wear no marine uniforms."

"What did they have on?"

"I hear they was dressed like frogmen, all in black."

"Merle, I'm scared," Booker said.

"Why?"

"They're all the same—the guys who came into Angaur, the guys who killed Elwell, the guys who planted Mo Kintaro down here. And my poachers, they were dressed in black. They're still around. You got a gun?"

"At the house. I got thirty years of guns."

"You got a boat?"

"At the dock in the village."

"We better get out of here, Merle, and off the island. They could be coming back."

They walked toward the nearest crawlway, the one where Rivera had died. Atkinson hopped into the hole and started pushing his way through. Then he stopped.

"What is it, Merle? Speak to me!" He was talking to the man's shoes. Booker grasped Atkinson's ankles and yanked him out of the pipe.

"It's no good," Atkinson announced. "There's someone comin' down the steps. I could see his flashlight."

"Sonofabitch!" Booker shouted. "Did they tell you to bring me down here? Is that what you talked about on the radio this morning? You're in on it!"

Before Atkinson could answer, Booker raced to the other open crawlway. He stuck his head inside the pipe, brought his flashlight forward, and switched it on.

The man who was kneeling outside blinked. And stared.

Now he ran toward the last exit, the one Atkinson had discovered. Booker started shoveling dirt with his hands, pulling obstructing rocks and boards out of the crawlway.

Atkinson stood beside him, arms akimbo. "You can knock it off," he said, tapping Booker on the shoulder. "You're not diggin' yourself out of this hole."

Booker turned around just in time to see the two poachers come crawling—no, flowing—out of the pipes that led into the headquarters.

They stood next to the crawlways like sentinels, each pointing a flashlight and a pistol at Marshall Booker.

A moment later, Major Scott Beckman followed. He motioned for Atkinson to sit down on a pile of Japanese debris stacked against the wall. Atkinson collapsed on a pile of crates and cradled his head between his knees, as if he were shaking off a hangover.

Beckman turned to Booker. "I looked for you at Atkinson's house. You were gone. That surprised me. They told me you'd headed out this way. That surprised me, too! What the hell are you doing down here?"

"I was about to ask you the same thing."

"Would you believe I came to get you out of here?"

"No, Major, I wouldn't believe that."

"You're right," Beckman said. "I didn't."

IV

Beckman gestured Booker across the room, toward where the first of the men in black was standing. He was tall, a little on the heavy side, but still muscular, like the catcher on a barroom softball team.

"Mother said that when you introduce people, you should always clearly give their names," Beckman said. "And then, after you give the names, you should tell them two or three significant things about each other. That way, if you get called away to another part of the room, they would have no problem carrying on a conversation while you're gone."

The man in black shifted impatiently, saying nothing. He had learned to tolerate Beckman's game-playing, it seemed.

"Well, this here's Marshall Booker," he told the sentinel. "He's from Amarillo, Texas, and Manhattan, and he's a journalist by trade. Right this minute, Mr. Booker's on assignment for *Gotham* magazine. Is there anything else I should add?"

Booker stood silent.

"Nothing more? Well then, this here is Private Leotis Murrell. Private Murrell is from Americus, Georgia, has served in Viet Nam, and now calls Guam his home. Over at the other crawlway, we have Corporal Jimmy Mack Edmunds of Oakland, California. Corporal Edmunds served in the Mekong. He's an adopted Guamanian, too. Both these gents reside in the Special Discharge Section. That special outfit you were so interested in. I promised to bring you together with a couple of 'em, remember?"

Beckman smiled at Booker.

"I take it there are no questions from the press. There's a third fellow who couldn't make it. You killed him yesterday. That was Sergeant Lewis Gomes of Providence, Rhode Island, our fun-loving Portugee. I should warn you that these fellows are wrought-up about that. They'd been through a lot together—war, crime, courts-martial, and rehabilitation. You wouldn't like what they've got planned for you. Unless you want to die with your pecker in your mouth."

Beckman paused a moment to let it all sink in, then turned to his escorts. "This fellow and I are gonna have a chat. He's mine. He makes a move, he's yours."

Beckman pushed Booker back toward the center of the room, to the wooden table where he and Atkinson had sat in darkness a few moments before.

"I want us to have a conversation," Beckman started. "I think . . ."

"Go to hell!"

"I want this to be a rational dialogue. Don't curse. And don't make me call in the night fighters."

Booker struggled to control his shaking.

"I'd like you to ask questions, and I'll answer them. After my opening statement. That's how I wanted us to spend this morning. Like a press conference. A not-for-attribution backgrounder."

There were these islands, Beckman began, tiny, meaningless specks of land lost in the Pacific. The islands of Micronesia had been discovered by accident, colonized by chance, captured in World War II as stepping stones to larger places—Okinawa and Japan. When peace came, the islands settled into a richly merited obscurity, the long yawn of the Trusteeship, the golden age of Thomas Dunbar.

But when the tide of American power which had swept over the islands began to dissipate twenty years later, ebbing and slipping backward across the Pacific, the little islands again began to matter.

They were safe places for Americans. Conquered once, conquered absolutely, they were havens for the men and equipment who were leaving Viet Nam, leaving Japan and Okinawa, beginning to worry about having to leave the Philippines. And there was no reason why America could not find shelter among the Micronesian islands. The long history of colonization, the lack of resources, the divided, scattered, backward population—all were ingredients for a happy client-state.

Micronesia could be had. And so, too, the Micronesians. With scholarships and uniforms. Trinkets and lines of credit. The promise of employment or travel. Junkets. A Lieutenant Pinkerton for every longing Angie. Buy a nation? Sure, when it totaled one hundred thousand people, half-trapped in the primitive world, half-nibbling at the twentieth century. It was easy.

Then Kintaro and a few others had returned, and Beckman knew he had a problem. In dismay, he watched the beginnings of the self-determination campaign. A lot of it was confusing. One day, Kintaro would orate about the old days in the islands, the classic folkways of Micronesia. He would rhapsodize about the independent ways of the outer islanders, who gathered all their own food, lived securely on their own islands, navigated the wide Pacific in hand-hewn outrigger canoes, steering by the stars. Then, the next day, Kintaro would be clamoring for paved roads, extended power and water lines, economic development, outside investment. One moment, the islanders ought to remain proud and self-sufficient; the next, the United States had better cough up a road grader, a sewage treatment plant, a whopping pay raise for Micronesian government employees.

Whatever he said, though, whether or not he meant what he said, Kintaro kept pounding away at the inconsistencies of American policy—that the United States had pledged to offer independence and at the same time had tied up the islands for future use as a chain of military bases. Up and down the territory he huffed and puffed, the sardonic, sad-eyed Palauan, belaboring "the neocolonial yoke under which we suffer." Before long, it seemed that every barfly and copra cutter could quote the embarrassing parts of the Trusteeship Agreement.

So Kintaro became Beckman's target—not to be killed, but to be disarmed, compromised. Elwell's drunken junket had been the lucky break. The "My Lai guys" had supplied a core of willing troops, and Mo Kintaro had been the unwitting weapon to be used, first against Elwell, and next—posthumously—against his own brother.

It had been a simple plan, Beckman said, and like all good plans, it left plenty of room for improvisation when things went wrong. Kintaro's brother, hired for an extravagant fifty dollars, was to halt Elwell's jeep and lead the victim down the trail. That was the end of his job and his knowledge. Somewhere in the thickets off the airfield, the My Lais would pounce and kill. Knives only. Then they would carry Elwell back to the jeep. The next morning he would be found, along with the corpse of his presumed slayer, Mo Kintaro. The world would be sad that Elwell had been murdered, delighted that he had had enough left to take his killer along with him, and outraged that the assassin was linked with a noisy politician who presumed to tell America how to run the islands its heroes had captured.

Atkinson, that idiot grotesque, had caught the My Lais in midstroke, sent them fleeing into Bloody Nose Ridge along with Mo Kintaro. But Beckman was ready to improvise. Down to Peleliu came war-loving Colonel Vincent, and the second battle for Bloody Nose Ridge began.

On Guam, Beckman had his share of anxious hours. Seven hundred miles south, hundreds of feet underground, were the My Lais and Mo Kintaro. He had to count on them to make the right moves—to escape from the caves and return to Angaur, while leaving Mo Kintaro behind. Meanwhile, Beckman had some moves of his own to make. As expected, Elwell's death had attracted a gaggle of reporters, more reporters than Guam had seen since Nixon's last stop. He wanted the whole pack of them out of there, off the island. But he also wanted one of them, just one, to remain behind. He was looking for someone he could work with, could involve in the story. Let him travel to Peleliu and play in the caves. Let him interview Kintaro, let him be Johnny-on-the-spot when they found Mo Kintaro. Let him make the connection between Elwell's probable murderer and the Palauan firebrand. And then, let him write his story. In the climate that followed, Kintaro and his people would be discredited as bloody, cynical thugs.

So he had gone shopping among the Fourth Estate, scanning the wrinkled suits and nicotined fingers, the double chins and hung-over faces. He preferred a word man to a picture man. And he wanted someone who was not under heavy deadline pressure. That left out the hard-news guys.

It was not easy. In the front rows were two men and one woman from the Guam newspapers. Small time. A man from *Stars and Stripes.* No good. Some Japanese correspondents from Tokyo. Ugh. *Time* and *Newsweek* correspondents, also from Tokyo, and some wire-service feature writers. Maybe. And an itinerant travel-feature writer from the *L.A. Times.* Maybe.

Ah, but then in the last row, he found just what he wanted. Feet up on a chair, pen in pocket, smirk on face, six feet of crotch and ego, his old buddy, Marshall Booker.

With Booker—a lazy reporter and an adroit stylist—the problem would be keeping him interested, keeping him around long enough for Mo to be found and identified and linked to his brother. Beckman had to sweeten the deal. So he teased him with the My Lai unit. Who could resist a story on an American Foreign Legion of misfit psychopath killers? The prospect of a My Lai exposé would keep Booker around. So much for the man's ego. That left his other parts. Inez could handle those.

V

"You're telling me you set this whole thing up to throw a penny-ante politician in jail?" Booker finally asked.

"Yes. And the irony is that tomorrow morning, I'm throwing that same penny-ante politician *out* of jail."

"What?"

"He caved. He abso-fucking-lutely caved! You should have been there! I walk into his cell and I can tell right away that Kintaro is loving every minute of it. He's surrounded himself with books, he's writing letters and memos, practically got posters of Che and Lumumba on the wall. Outside, you could see his little punks holding protest signs. 'Coconut Power.' 'No More War in Our Islands.' 'Give Us Our Land.' 'Elwell Was the Last.'

"So I let him rattle on for a few minutes. It's all bullshit. Talk about monkeys coming out of trees! I listen politely. I sit there and take it. Finally, when he runs out of breath, I let him know what we've got on him. The substance of it being two hundred and sixty pounds of his family, found in a cave, frozen, and stored in a food locker on Angaur.

"Then I point to the punks in the street, Elwell's name on their placards. I point to the books, the manuscripts, the whole little tableau of imprisonment. I gently suggest that he set up Elwell to put some juice into his humpty-dumpty independence crusade. I even quote some passages from his oratory at the high school. You should've been there. I was a regular district attorney."

"Eloquent bastard when you want to be."

"What followed was even more eloquent. Eloquent as only silence can be, five minutes of it. Him sitting there in that cell, those sad brown eyes staring at me. When Kintaro begins talking to me, he is not rhetorical or political. He is back about a quarter of a century, before he ran for office, before we sent him off to school, before we taught him political science—hell, before we taught him English. He is suddenly a scared little kid on a dock again, watching boatloads of tall, blond god-men landing an LST at his muddy little village, and him standing there on the dock, wide-eyed.

"And then he caves in. He as much as tells me that his whole movement was mostly talk. His whole point wasn't going independent—only jacking up the prices for military land sales and leases. To hang tough, drive a hard bargain. Kintaro's no revolutionary. He's a broker-realtor. And he doesn't want to build an island nation. He wants to sell one, at the highest possible price. When the time comes to deal, he'll deal. We'll get our bases, with no crying towels in front of the United Nations."

Beckman fell silent. Along with his satisfaction at having bested a foe, he seemed downcast that his foe had collapsed so readily. This diminished his victory, Beckman seemed to feel. The cause had not been so worthwhile nor the enemy so formidable as he had hoped. They were small islands, after all, and island people, and Beckman was still playing in the minor leagues. He had defused a powder keg, and it turned out to be a pork barrel.

"Then why do this . . . why do anything to me? You've already won!"

"You know too much," Beckman said. "Look at you down here, poking around for clues with this Atkinson asshole."

"I won't write the story! I'll kill it!"

"That just won't do. I've already thought about it. You make a promise here. So what about when you get back to New York?"

"Trust me!"

"You wouldn't trust me, if we turned it around."

"But it doesn't make any sense! It doesn't add up! I get killed so's Uncle Sam can grab off the Rinky-Dink Islands? From people who wanted them grabbed off in the first place?"

"I *am* sorry about that," Beckman said, sounding as if he meant it. "But we didn't know about Kintaro, how serious a threat he was. We had to be sure about him. And now we have to be sure about you. That's why I sent the boys down yesterday. And today, finding you down here, I'm surer than ever that you have to go."

"It's grotesque! You cook up this whole scheme to compromise a guy who *might* be pushing independence. But he wasn't. And still, I have to die. The waste!"

"On the contrary," Beckman said, "this operation has been a model of economy. Fifteen hundred American boys died on Peleliu. Just lousy Peleliu! Three thousand more on Saipan! Hundreds of others on Tinian and Angaur and Kwaj and Eniwetok, not counting the ones who drowned or got shot down. That should have been enough. You've seen these islands—wasn't that enough of a price to pay? But the prevailing fools left a loophole. They put the islands under the U.N. They made promises they shouldn't have made; they raised false expectations. They taught these guys political science. They should've taught them farming. Well, finally it became necessary to mount a little operation that would finish up the winning of the islands. And—this is *beautiful*—who comes back to do the job? Who comes back for the mop-up? Red Elwell! Who should have died here in the first place!"

"You're crazy . . . crazy as Colonel Vincent."

"Vincent was still fighting Double-U Double-U Two. Not me. At the cost of a couple Americans—a My Lai guy, an Elwell, a Booker, or so—I wrap it up. I save hundreds of American lives, maybe. Buddy mine, I should be up for peace prizes!"

"You'd kill me, peacemaker?"

"It's a damned shame. I took a chance with you, fifty-fifty, and we lost. If Kintaro hadn't caved, you'd have your story. But he caved in, and you started snooping. So we lose the story. We lose you. Sorry about that."

"Go to hell!"

"Your whole vocabulary comes down to *that?*"

"You and your strategic circle jerks."

"I expected better from you. Reason and logic instead of obscenities."

"You're prolonging this! You sadistic prick, you love it!"

"Perhaps I do. Less now than before, though. There's going to be one more accident inside this old mountain. One whopper of an explosion. Folks will assume that

Uncle Merle let one slip. After that, we'll seal this death trap off. Ten, twenty years from now, maybe we'll let the Japs dig their way in to you."

"You'll be here, too." It was Merle Atkinson, all but forgotten in this talk of old wars and new. Three flashlights moved to where he was sitting against the wall. The lanky hillbilly was in the spotlight, and he was smiling.

"We'll all be here together."

Out of the crates he'd been sitting on, Atkinson slowly hefted two hunks of metal, brown and pear-shaped. He cradled them gently in the palm of one hand, while he hooked the fingers of his other hand around the tops, as if he were plucking stems off fruit.

"These may look like Jap grenades, Major Beckman. They feel like Jap grenades. But don't be fooled. These are your balls I'm holding in my hand."

"You're bluffing."

"Try me."

"After twenty-five years, they're harmless."

"There's a lot of one-armed men around these islands could tell you otherwise. And some dead ones would if they could. Want to try me?"

"What's the deal?"

"I want you off of this here island. Up the steps we go, all of us, all the way to the dock."

"We keep our guns. I won't disarm."

"Keep 'em. But stay close."

They were at the dock. The two My Lai guys were already in the boat, the motors idling. Atkinson was watching them closely. In addition to the grenades, he now had produced a pistol from under the seat of his jeep. Insurance, he said.

"You won this battle," Beckman conceded. "Not the war."

"I fight one battle at a time," Atkinson answered. "You decide about the war."

"Are you going to keep your mouth shut?"

"Yeah. So long as no one presses me."

"How about you, Booker?"

"How about me?"

"You going to write the story?"

"Just the way it happened. With smoke coming off my typewriter."

"I wish you wouldn't do that. This My Lai unit has graduates. And some indebted, highly active alumni, all over the place. You'd be surprised."

"No deal."

"We do need these islands. And Kintaro did appear a valid threat. National security . . ."

"Cut the crap," Atkinson interrupted. "And get in the damned boat."

Beckman shrugged and embarked. The boat quickly sprinted over fifty yards of water, racing for Angaur. Booker turned to thank—to embrace—Merle Atkinson.

"One thousand one, one thousand two . . ."

The grenade sailed across the water. Beckman shouted, and they all dove onto the floor of the boat.

". . . one thousand and three . . . oh, hell."

The grenade plopped harmlessly into the water.

"Japanese grenades never were worth shit," Merle Atkinson said. "No wonder they lost the war."

TEN
EPILOGUE

No one had bothered to do him harm.

When the killing had ended, the politics and scheming, Thomas Dunbar remained behind in the district administrator's residence—the rambling, leaking house on the hill above the islands and the sea.

He had put in his years, they told him. He was close to retirement, and all he had to worry about was not making waves.

Unnecessarily, Dunbar went to his office daily and shuffled cables: road repairs, passport matters, pest control. He sometimes met the planes that flew down from Guam and Saipan. He checked progress on the jumbo runways they were cutting into the jungle on Babelthuap. He surveyed the dredging operations that were deepening and widening Malakal harbor.

At night, he sat down to dinner with his wife and children, the long table of Palauan food, the soup from taro sprouts, broiled fish and fried breadfruit, soursop and papaya, the dash of rum in coconut juice. When the table was cleared, his wife adjourned to the kitchen to join his Palauan in-laws, and Dunbar listened to the alien chatter he so missed whenever he left home.

Most of the people who had entered his world and torn it apart were gone now, and he was left alone to preside over the fencing, the dredging, the paving of Palau.

Elwell had gone first, in a flag-draped coffin. A couple of marines had followed him that way. Then Colonel Vincent had decamped, as good as dead.

Beckman drifted back and forth, supervising preparations for the new bases. Francisco Kintaro was still around, but not for long. A State Department "Young Leaders' Grant" would soon transport him to the Virgin Islands, Puerto Rico, American Samoa, and Hawaii. All United States territories, past and present.

Atkinson had more or less disappeared. Finished on Peleliu, he had been scheduled for assignment in the Truk District, where piric acid had been leaking out of depth charges in a sunken Japanese freighter, threatening the marine life in the lagoon. But Atkinson never showed up for work in Truk. The distad assumed that he had found a better deal someplace else.

Marshall Booker was the real puzzler. The last time he had passed through Koror, the journalist had stayed at the distad's house. He said the hotels were full—a patent lie—but the distad did not mind putting him up so he could save a little money on expenses. At that time, Booker had seemed all full of a story that would really shake things up in the Trust Territory. The Pentagon, the Department of Interior, the Micronesians themselves—no one would be spared, or so Booker had hinted.

The distad waited and waited for the article to appear. *Gotham* arrived late anyway. Sometimes, nothing for weeks on end, then three or four copies, all in a bunch. He looked through them from cover to cover and found nothing. He had almost decided that the article had not worked out. It did not surprise him. The islands were always being "discovered" by new writers who got flushed with excitement, only to return home and learn that no one really wanted to read about such a small and faraway place.

The distad had given up on Marshall Booker and was leafing through *Gotham,* looking at the advertisements, when he found what had happened to Booker's article.

> Marshall Booker drowned off a beach in Hawaii last week. At his death, the talented young Texas-born journalist was completing a *Gotham* assignment on the death of Lewis "Red" Elwell in Micronesia some time ago. The Elwell piece—uncompleted at Booker's death—was his first assignment for this magazine, but it would not have been his last. His energy and humor had already revealed themselves in dozens of other pieces, most of which have been collected in two books, *Down Home* and *One Night Stands.* We will miss Marshall Booker at this magazine. Though he was not given the time to fill these pages, he surely had the talent.—Edmund Shank

Only Dunbar remained. And lately, he had convinced himself that remaining was the only thing that mattered. Finding a place in the world and staying there, staying in a place you loved, staying even when you loved it less than before, and found less in it to love.

Everyone else came and went. Americans. Japanese. And Palauans, no exception to this awful transience. The islands had grown too small for the islanders.

Maybe you could not blame them for leaving. It was a small place in which to live your life, to bury yourself away. But he knew something that the Palauans were only learning: that the world was small, itself an island full of islands, in a sky of islands.

Every night, before the mosquitoes came, he sat on his lawn and looked at the skyful of stars. And every night, the metaphor came true.